Giel Boy

18664364957

DARK STORM RISING

CHINELU MOORE

Genesis Press, Inc.

Indigo Love Stories

An imprint of Genesis Press, Inc.
Publishing Company

Genesis Press, Inc.
P.O. Box 101
Columbus, MS 39703

ISBN-13: 978-1-58571-312-7
ISBN-10: 1-58571-312-0
Manufactured in the United States of America

First Edition 1996
Second Edition 2008

Visit us at www.genesis-press.com or call at 1-888-Indigo-1

CHAPTER 1

Starmaine Lassiter stretched her long-limbed body to the sonorous strains of Whitney's "Saving All My Love." She crooned the song's lyrics and laughed when her voice veered off-key. "Yep, the only thing Whitney and I have in common is we sort of look like each other," she said aloud.

She liked to begin her aerobics warm-up with a slow beat and then later switch to a quicker tempo for the rest of her daily hour-long workout. As she used to tell the aerobics students she'd taught at various spas and resorts, "Exercise doesn't have to be a pain. It's all in the way you think about it. After a while, exercise becomes just another thing you do as a part of your daily regimen—like taking a shower or brushing your teeth."

Of course, most people didn't need to work out for an hour a day, but in her job as a fitness designer who developed exercise programs for spas, resorts, and fitness centers, she had to stay in top form.

Star realized it was nearly one o'clock. With any luck, she'd be completely finished with her routine before she heard the baby's lunchtime whimpers coming through the intercom speaker that transmitted all sounds from the nursery throughout the house. Little Nanette always whimpered before she wailed.

Star moved into a wide-legged stance and prepared to do a thigh-firming exercise she'd learned in a karate class in college. As she did this, a large shadow crossed the sun-flecked room. Her head swiveled to the source of the intruding shape.

A man's form parted the dense, tall evergreen bushes that screened the largely glass room. Her hands shaded her eyes to dim the sudden blast of light, but momentarily blinded by the bright sun, she couldn't see his face. She could only tell that he was dark and too tall to be her brother-in-law Larry. Besides, why would Larry be looking through the shrubbery when he could come in through one of the several doors of the house? Could it be a peeping Tom? She'd always assumed they operated at night.

These thoughts flashed through her mind in a split second, and feeling safely enclosed inside the room, she padded across the white sisal-carpeted room to where the intruder stood, still peering through one of the long windows.

A feeling of extreme annoyance shot through her. Why was he standing there looking into a private home? As she reached the window, she stood to the side so she could see him better. Her supersensitive eyes were still having trouble adjusting to the light.

"Yes?" she queried without hiding her annoyance.

"I rang the doorbell, but no one answered," he responded.

"Yes?" she tried again.

"I told Larry I would drop off these in-ground lights." His head nodded toward a bag he held. "If I could find them," he shouted in order to be heard through the double-paned glass that separated them.

"Oh," she said, changing her annoyed and suspicious tone to a more pleasant one, even giving him a small smile. "Go around. I'll open the garage and you can put them there."

He smiled and disappeared in the direction of the garage.

As Star slid open the patio door, she heard Nanette's wail. The baby, undoubtedly awakened by the man's shouting, must have already gone through the first stages of her lunch request.

"Auntie's coming," Star called out as she bounded up the stairs to the baby's room. Normally, Little Nanette was a happy, gurgling child, but if she wasn't fed on time, she would be uncomfortable and very grumpy for the rest of the afternoon and evening.

Star knew her sister Gail would not be in the mood for a bad-tempered daughter, no matter how adorable—not after dealing with the squabbles and tantrums of the special education students in her class.

She picked up the thrashing baby and cuddled her, talking to her in soothing tones as she quickly brought her down the stairs to the kitchen.

Just as she stuck the bottle with its warmed contents into the furious child's mouth, she heard the front doorbell chime and simultaneously remembered the man.

She hurried toward the door, holding the child in her arms. Opening it, she noticed the irritation on the man's face, but when he saw the baby, his expression became pleasant.

"I wondered what was taking so long." His voice was deep and he spoke with an accent that she couldn't identify. He was thirtyish, good-looking and somehow familiar. Her brow furrowed as she tried to remember where she'd seen him before. His eyes were familiar.

"You're the man from Pathmark!" She suddenly recalled an incident a few nights ago when a galling man in a grimy uniform had pushed her grocery cart out of the line. She'd left it to hunt for some tomato paste and, well, a few other items. When she returned, her shopping cart had been pushed aside and there he stood in its place as the clerk rang up his purchases. Luckily, no one else was in the line, so she pushed her cart almost on his heels.

"Excuse me, but I was in line here," she had snapped loudly.

His head had pivoted toward her, and his eyes had given her a quick once-over before he replied. "No, you weren't in line; a cart was here. If you weren't ready to stand in line, you shouldn't have put the cart in line," he'd said, lecturing her in a foreign accent.

Furious, she had thrown back her head, refusing look at him as the clerk packed his boxes of garbage bags and giant-sized packages of paper towels.

Before she turned away from him, she'd seen a glint of amusement in his arresting eyes—eyes the color of wine tinged with brown.

What she wanted to do was ram her cart right into him. As satisfying as that might have been, it would have been risky, so she contented herself with silently jabbing him.

He's just a janitor who makes pathetic power plays by jumping lines at the supermarket, she thought as she recalled how he had brazenly looked her up and down. Of course this was to be totally expected of a man so rude. How like such a man! She almost laughed aloud.

Now he stood before her talking about Larry and in-ground lights.

"I stand accused." He laughed, crossing his chest with his arms. "I'm Daran Ajero. I live across the way," he said, indicating a large house backed by acres of farmland.

"You mean over there?" she said, darting her head in the direction of one of the largest homes in the Blueberry Farms development.

The house she referred to was a huge two-story wheat-colored brick structure with shuttered black Palladiun windows and two sets of French patio doors at the back. From the main highway, the back of the house looked awesome in the distance because of its two-tiered patio, which connected the top level to the lower one by a curved black wrought-iron staircase. One could get a glimpse only while driving by, however. Thick clumps of trees shielded much of the house. Actually, the closer you got to it, the less you saw of it.

"Yes, my house was the second house built in this development." As if reading her mind, he continued. "The land was a steal then, so I put a lot of money into building the house I wanted instead of paying triple the price for the land. It would cost me twice as much now."

Star nodded, enjoying the musical cadence of his speech.

"Larry must've told you about me?" he inquired, cocking his head to one side.

"You know how Larry is," she dodged. She smiled and hoped this reference to her notoriously absent-minded brother-in-law would explain why she knew nothing about this man.

He continued. "It took me a while to convince Larry that buying the land and building his house made the best of sense, especially after he'd become a husband."

Star noticed that his warm, wine-colored eyes appeared to be smiling even when there was no smile on his face. She watched his eyes study her face and swiftly drop to her long, bare thighs and legs. She then remembered what she wearing: a hot pink leotard with a scoop neck and an attached flared skirt that accentuated the roundness of her thighs. Normally she felt completely comfortable in the outfit. It was for her a typical work uniform. But this man's eyes made her warm. With her free hand, she tugged the short skirt but to no avail.

She surprised herself again when she heard her voice say in the most neighborly tone she could summon, "Why don't you have a seat? I'm Starmaine."

It was a warm late September day and the veranda running across the front of the house was shady. He sat in one of the wooden Colonial two-seaters that flanked the left side of the front door. She eased herself down into a matching one across from him, still holding Nanette. The baby's chubby hands still clutched the bottle, though she had finished its contents. Maybe the air will soothe her, Star thought, as she gazed down fondly at her little niece.

"Well, I'll just stay for a minute," he said, his eyes meeting hers directly as he smiled fully for the first time. Star noticed a gap between his front upper teeth. It only enhanced his looks. He folded his tall, muscular body onto the chair and leaned forward, placing his elbows on his thighs, which bulged through his well-cut beige slacks. His salmon-colored polo shirt complemented his dark chocolate skin.

"I'm sorry I missed Larry's wedding—your wedding. It must have been heavenly, considering the bride." She smiled, accepting the compliment. Her eyes inspected him as she spoke.

"Well it was a small affair actually," she said conversationally, omitting that she had not been the bride. She was enjoying the pretense of being Larry's wife. It was only fair. The guy had one-upped her at the grocery store and she was getting back at him. At some future point, the two families would have a good laugh about it.

"How do you like your new home?" he asked, his smiling eyes running down her neck to the bare skin above her breasts.

Star bristled at his marauding eyes. The nerve of him to openly ogle her—a woman he thought was married, and married to his friend, no less! Down, girl, she warned herself as a scorching remark almost spilled from her lips. He is Larry's friend and, evidently, a foreigner. She'd always heard that foreign men were very bold with their hands, and with their eyes too, apparently.

"Oh, it's tons of work, of course. Men don't know what it's like having to find just the right window treatments to match the light and mood of the room, and everything is so expensive," she answered him, repeating what she'd heard Gail say to Larry two nights before on the phone. "Your wife must've had fits decorating your huge place, or did you have a decorator come in?"

He smiled again, showing even white teeth and red gums that contrasted vividly with his dark skin. "There is no wife, and yes, I did have a decorator come in to do some of the rooms. I needed some of them done for my clients."

The fact that he wasn't married both shocked and pleased her. She covered up these emotions by blurting, "Clients? What type of clients?" Her brain thumbed through all the occupations in which one would have clients.

He regarded her quizzically, his gaze resting on her lips, which had parted in surprise. "Larry really didn't tell you anything about me, did he?"

Star's heart lurched. Pretty soon he'd find out she was an impostor. Considering Larry's relationship with Daran, surely she should know more about the guy than she did. She needed to bring this little chat to an end.

She stood up, saying, "Well, you should know by now Larry is extremely absentminded. He's a brilliant engineer, but other things escape him. Besides," she rambled on, "he moved everything in here all by himself. We got here just one day before school opened, and things have been crazy ever since. Settling into a new house is no joke."

Star knew she was babbling and had to force herself to stop. The combination of his probing eyes and prodding questions had put her on extreme alert. Her pulse raced as his eyes caressed every spot on her body. She feared he would soon know the effect he was having on her. The whole situation had become too uncomfortable.

Daran noticed the sudden change in her and the look of alarm that had settled in her eyes. Damn it! He cursed himself. She's nervous. My eyes must have betrayed my thoughts. What a honey-colored beauty! Damn Larry!

Star stood up. "It's certainly been nice chatting with you but I've got to get the baby to bed."

They both looked at the snoozing baby, who could not have been less concerned about her whereabouts. But Star's abrupt movement caused the baby's empty bottle to fall, bounce off Star's bare foot, and skitter beneath the two-seater.

"Let me," he said, bending swiftly to retrieve it before she could move out of the way.

He crouched between her legs and she could not move unless she tried to step over him—a dangerous feat, considering she still held the baby.

As Daran reached for the bottle, his face was within inches of Star's long legs. Legs that curved delicately upward to her firm thighs. He could smell her slightly sweaty female scent, wafting through the air around him and he became light-headed and aroused all at once. He closed his eyes and inhaled her, knowing the moment would imprint on his brain. His lips yearned to kiss her calf and travel on up. He clenched his jaw to get control of himself. She was a married woman! Larry's wife! He couldn't help the effect this woman was having on him, but he could certainly restrain himself. He hated adulterers!

Star felt the heat of his breath on her legs and began to sweat. A tingling feeling started at the pit of her stomach and crept down to her toes. Her knees became weak. She felt they could give out at any moment and she would fall, taking the baby with her.

Just as he was rising, she moved slightly and his face brushed the soft flesh of her upper thighs.

She let out a little scream and began to fall backward into the chair. He clutched her arms to break her fall, easing her and the still-sleeping child into the chair.

Closing her eyes, she let out a long sigh, completely shaken.

The riveting impact of the exchange stunned him, too, for a few seconds. Then he became aware of how his muscles ached from holding his body in check. But he recovered himself before she did.

"I'm sorry," he heard himself say. "Are you all right?" Before she could answer, they both heard the sound of a vehicle on the road near the veranda.

They both turned to see a black pickup truck stop abruptly. A small, buxom woman dressed in a peach-colored dress stepped from it. She beckoned to Daran. "There's an urgent phone call for you. Luckily, I saw your car over here. Hurry!"

As he moved from the veranda, he glanced at Star. His eyes held no laughter now. Instead they contained a look no woman could mistake.

As Star prepared dinner late that afternoon, she still reeled from the day's events and her own puzzling reactions to them. She couldn't wait for Gail to come home. Questions abounded about this neighbor— Larry's good friend Daran.

Gail finally arrived at four-thirty, but instead of bombarding her with questions about the man, Star retreated to safer ground. "When's Larry coming home?" she asked chattily.

Gail sighed, "Not 'til the end of the month. Can you believe that?" Gail's usually cherubic face was downcast as she raked the last of the meat and vegetable mixture from the blender into a bowl for Nanette's dinner.

Then she shrugged and smiled as she continued, "I tell you, Star. I think that company wants to adopt my husband. First, he was just supposed to oversee the installation of a new food tower in their plant in Ireland. That was two weeks ago! Then the company decided that since he was already over there, he might as well make a quick dip into Africa and inspect their Egyptian facility. He did that. Now guess what's happened?"

"What?" Star asked as she plopped some chicken wings into the microwave to thaw. She could tell from the scowl that ran from Gail's thick eyebrows to her small pointed chin that Larry's employer had reached new heights of audacious behavior.

"Oh, they want him to stay on to discuss some new inspection procedures with two managers who are currently on vacation!" Gail's large, dark eyes blazed as she recounted this last galling bit.

Star chuckled, and her sister shot her a withering glare.

"Really, Star. What's funny about this situation? I got married to have a husband. Not to be a lonely wife and single mother parked out in the country!"

"Well, how much longer does he have to stay?"

"He doesn't know yet." Gail shut her eyes tightly, pressing back hot tears of disappointment.

Realizing there was nothing she could say to make Gail feel less bad about Larry's postponed return, Star busied herself seasoning the thawed chicken. But moments later she broke into laughter and pointed at Nanette. The baby had pulled herself up out of her high chair determined to reach the spoonful of food that Gail, now gazing out the window, held just inches from the child's mouth.

Seeing what was happening and the humor of it all, Gail began to laugh. "See what I mean. Now that company's causing me to neglect my child!" She turned to Nanette and continued to feed her.

Star came over to the counter island and perched on a stool across from her older sister. "Get a grip on yourself, Gail. You're just lonely, and that's caused you to run off at the mouth. You know Larry loves that kind of responsibility, and he's being paid a heck of a lot of money. Both of you knew he'd be traveling sixty percent of the time. The company told you that back at square one. Remember? You told me that."

Gail put her hand on her hip and rolled her eyes at her younger sister. "Whose side are you on anyway, Starmaine?" she asked, only half kidding.

Star knew she ran the risk of getting Gail more upset, but she also knew her sister could make the biggest mountain out of a molehill if she wasn't stopped in time. With this in mind, Star smiled and continued.

"I also remember that Larry had some serious reservations about taking this job, but you egged him on. Furthermore, you and Nanette could be with him. You told me, remember? You told me even before Larry took the job that it had a provision allowing the spouse and children to travel along a certain percentage of the time. That was one of the perks that made him decide to take the job. But you chose to stay here and be aggravated by your darling students." Then mimicking her sister, Star added, "We'll travel with him during the summer break."

A wry expression came over Gail's face. Then she smiled. "Oh, don't remember everything I say, and don't be so darn right all the time," she said, flicking an imaginary piece of food at Star.

"Gailee," Star said, reverting to her sister's pet name, "I know you miss him, but you can't go around here dragging your chin on the floor, feeling sorry for yourself. I know how you are. You are the original Miss Magnify. Pretty soon everything will be so big in your mind you'll think Larry's staying away from home deliberately."

"Okay, little sister, you've made your point," Gail said as she cleaned up the spotty mess from the floor around the high chair. "I know Larry loves me, but sometimes I just need him around to rub my feet and—"

Grimacing comically, Star interrupted. "Kindly spare me all the lurid details."

She slid the chicken into the oven as thoughts of that man with the laughing eyes paraded through her mind again, accompanied by a host of busy butterflies in her stomach. She wondered how she could casually tell Gail about the unnerving events of the day.

Could she nonchalantly tell her that she'd been turned into a mass of panting, quivering jelly by a neighbor who had stopped by? Or would she begin by saying that for the first time she understood why some women had quickies with the deliveryman?

Pretending to check out whether Daran Ajero was Larry's friend or some nut gave her the pretext to open the dam of questions. "Oh, a guy who said he's a friend of Larry's came by today and dropped off some lights," Star began, and then realized she didn't know where the lights were because she'd never gotten around to opening the garage. Had he left them on the front porch?

"A friend of Larry's?" Gail queried, dumbfounded for a moment. "Oh that must have been the African guy who lives over there, Larry's friend, hm. What's his name?"

"Daran Ajero," Star answered, supplying the name.

Gail stood up and rinsed her hands off at the sink in the kitchen island. "Do you know I've never met him? What's he like?" Gail asked.

Before Star could answer, Nanette began coughing on her fruit juice. Gail became too busy patting the little girl's back to notice Star's difficulty in answering this simple question.

It wasn't until Gail had the baby soothed and had transferred her to her play area in the family room that she picked up the thread of their conversation again. "So what's he like? What time did he come by?"

Star was relieved she had her back to Gail as she answered. Her voice suddenly didn't sound normal. "Oh, he's tall and on the slim side," she said. But very muscular, she thought as she rubbed and squeezed the smooth flesh of a cucumber under the running water.

"Larry says he's brilliant and a very sharp businessman. He gave Larry some very good investment advice a few years ago, and now my husband—you know how he is—he swears by Daran."

"Hm," Star intoned noncommittally. "Larry says he's charming—and can talk the skin off a grape!"

A fresh swarm of butterflies attacked Star's stomach as she recalled the way his eyes had moved over her. His lips had mouthed only polite and proper pleasantries, but his eyes had let the real message slip.

"As a matter of fact, if it hadn't been for him, Larry would have never bought this land and we wouldn't be standing in this house right now."

Star gave her sister a puzzled look.

Gail munched on some melon cubes as she explained. "Larry and Daran met at a Black Student Union meeting at M.I.T. and became very good friends. After college, though, they kind of fell out of touch. Then a few years ago, they met again at some sort of conference. It was when Larry had just gotten his first engineering job. That was right before I met Larry. I remember Larry telling me, maybe on our second date, that he'd recently run into an African friend who'd just been recruited for a high-level engineering position by an oil company in Africa. Larry even said he'd thought about working in Africa himself one day."

Gail paused and a smile flickered over her heart-shaped face. "It just occurred to me that he will be working in Africa, at least for the few days when he goes to Egypt. Anyway, that's why I remember the conversation. It got me to wondering what it'd be like to live and work over there."

"But what's that got to do with Larry buying this land?" Star blurted. She knew it could take her long-winded sister until tomorrow to get to the here and now.

"Okay, I'm getting there," Gail said, gesturing for Star to be patient. "Well, Larry and I got married later that year. And I started noticing that Larry would sometimes get letters from Nigeria, from Daran, and he'd mention to me that Daran was fine and dah-dah-dah-dah-dah. About a year or so later, Larry told me that Daran had left the oil company and started his own business. He wanted Larry to be his consultant and agent over here, since the business involved buying industrial equipment for African businessmen who were setting up manufacturing companies. Well, Larry tried but it didn't work out. He just didn't have the time. Anyway, the next thing I heard was Daran had married an African American who was living in Nigeria. By this time he'd become very successful. But his wife wanted to go back home, since Daran was spending a lot of time on business trips either to Europe or the United States. So they moved to New York, and Daran and Larry would get together whenever Larry was in New York and Daran was in town."

"But why didn't you ever meet him? Didn't you at least talk to him?" Star asked, recalling her early afternoon charade as Larry's wife.

"I talked to him once when he called from Nigeria, but the connection was bad. Our voices were echoing. It was like we were talking through a tunnel. Besides, I knew the call was very expensive, so I quickly gave the phone back to Larry."

Gail was interrupted by the sound of one of the pots on the stove as its lid plopped up and down. She started for the stove.

Star headed her off. "Now you just go sit down. When I'm here all day, I take care of the cooking, remember?"

"Oh honey, you know just what to say to me!" Gail said, as she sashayed to the kitchen's long window seat and lay back daintily.

"Anywa-ay. Let's see. Where was I?" "You were telling me why you'd never met him," Star prompted, "and how he led you to this lot."

"Oh, once when Larry met him in New York, he told Larry he planned to invest some money in farmland in Delaware. He was just speculating and thought maybe Larry would want to come in with him on the deal. Larry wanted to, but we couldn't afford it at the time. Within a year, Daran had sold ten of the fifteen acres he bought—ones over there around his house. He kept the other five for his own estate."

"Well, I am impressed," Star said, thinking, A hunk with brains, I do declare.

"I think sometimes he uses some of his clients' money," Gail said dramatically in a loud stage whisper, though there wasn't a chance anyone could hear her.

"Well, nobody ever said that making big money is a saintly activity. Look at some of the richest folks in this country now. Some of their ancestors rolled in the dirt to get that money and now…" Star stopped, suddenly realizing she sounded like she was defending him.

"Whoa! Whoa!" Gail said and looked at her for a moment. "I don't think he needs a defense lawyer yet.

I wasn't accusing him of anything or criticizing him. It was just something Larry told me."

"Don't pay me any attention, Gailee. You know me. I always root for the underdog."

"This guy is no underdog. Nobody takes advantage of him, at least not in business," Gail said, and then she paused.

"What do you mean by that?" Star asked, setting bowls of salad on the table and beckoning her sister over.

"Well, Larry said Daran's wife was real dirty to him. She really hurt him." Gail spooned some blue cheese dressing on the vegetable salad and began to eat.

"Sounds like that's the past. What's going on with them now?" Star asked, recalling his words: There is no wife.

"Oh, nothing, I don't think. They got a divorce." Chuckling, she added, "I can't believe how much I know about this guy and I wouldn't know him from Adam if I met him on the street."

Star was silent. She remembered the buxom woman who'd come to get him earlier. Who was she?

Throughout dinner, Gail chattered on about when and how she and Larry had decided to buy the land and build their home, but Star only half listened.

She kept touching the spot on her bare thigh where Daran Ajero's lips had seared her skin. The spot still tingled.

CHAPTER 2

The rain spattered the Philadelphia sidewalks while wind whipped all around. Star gripped the handle of her umbrella. Every few moments it threatened to turn into a parachute, so fierce was the wind. With her free hand, she tightened the belt of her shiny black raincoat.

She loved the coat. Its padded epaulet shoulders, large pockets, long length, and roomy fit gave it a sleek, stylish appearance and made it all-purpose.

Fortunately she'd zipped in the quilted lining today because the wind and rain gave the early October air a nasty chill. And beneath the coat, she wore only a body suit, her work uniform, covered by a short denim skirt.

She made a reckless dash across the street, cutting in front of a slew of oncoming taxis, and then ducked into the huge Placido building. Within the atrium lobby, people talked and strolled or waited with glum faces for the rain to cease.

The elevator whisked Star to the top floor—home to the Placido Fitness Club and Health Arena. The elevator doors opened onto a plush environment exquisitely designed to welcome, comfort, and stimulate. The decor did its job admirably. Each time Star stepped off the elevator, she felt she was entering an opulent oasis. Thick salmon-colored Aubusson rugs covered the vast entrance and lounging area. Tulip-shaped chairs in matching hues were arranged to provide seating areas set off by large exotic plants that gave a degree of privacy while offering a view of the lobby. To Star's left stood the S-shaped information and registration counter. She headed there now to pick up her messages.

As the fitness program designer and consultant for the Philadelphia Placido, Star was headquartered here, but she also acted as an on-call consultant for three other Placido health clubs in the Delaware Valley chain. As the Philadelphia club was the first and by far the largest, it received the bulk of her time. It also contained the Placida's executive offices. Star's own office here was equipped with a shower stall and a large, adjoining dressing room.

"Hi, Star," the redheaded receptionist greeted her.

"Hi, Deidra. How's it going?"

"Oh, the usual." The girl stuck the eraser end of her pencil between her teeth. "Let me just double-check to make sure these are all your messages. I got yelled at the other day for mixing some of them up." She leaned forward and lowered her voice conspiratorially before launching into some juicy gossip involving the confused messages.

Star took it in stride, being used to Deidra's love of health-club intrigue. She half listened, enjoying Deidra's pleasure in telling the story more than the story itself.

Once the girl had finished, she handed Star a sheaf of messages.

Still shaking her head and chuckling, Star shuffled through the color-coded messages. The color indicated which of the four locations the message was from.

Nothing earth-shattering, she noted, as she flipped through the paper squares. A buff-colored message—Placido's Philly color—was from Rex, the club's equipment and facilities director. Just seeing his name, scrawled in Deidra's handwriting, gave Star a good feeling. She'd been friends with Rex for years and was looking forward to having dinner with him that night.

Only two other messages—mint green, indicating Placido Wilmington—held her attention. Both were from women who wanted more information about a women's health and support group Star was forming.

Six weeks before, while at the Wilmington location, she'd expressed her support for that club's quite unique holistic approach to fitness and health. After endorsing the club's approach, she'd said the time had come to recognize that good health encompassed all aspects of a person's life—not just the physical but the emotional as well. She'd spoken to a small group of women there, telling them how she had tried once before to organize a women's health and support group and that she believed the time was right to try it again. The women had heartily agreed that her idea was right on time. Star's spirits lifted as she read messages from two of those Wilmington women. A long-distance call meant more than a passing interest in the support group—a project that had quickly become Star's favorite. The first meeting was scheduled for the next day at a Wilmington community center.

Star had picked the location to reach as many women as possible, whether they belonged to the elite Placido club or not. Reminded of the inaugural meeting, Star felt both nervous and excited. But right now she needed to get to work.

"Is Christina in her office?" she asked Deidra, wanting, as usual, to check in with the club's operations manager. With Star's question, Deidra once more leaned forward, getting ready to deliver more gossip. "Oh, she left at noon with Quint." Deidra arched her right eyebrow pointedly.

"And she said she had another meeting after lunch." The redhead stared into Star's eyes to make sure her meaning hit home.

The woman was so obvious Star could not contain herself. She laughed aloud and wagged her finger in the receptionist's face. "Deidra, if I ever get a love life, I'll make sure I keep a lot of distance between it and you."

"Well, there's no point in being cute about these things. They almost left here running. Now do I or do I not look like I'm a day old?" she asked.

"Deidra, Deidra," Star said, shaking her head with good-natured amazement. "What are we going to do with you?" She paused to let her point sink in before adding, "Anyway, I'm off to Arena One. Let me know if I get any calls."

Luckily, the phone began to ring again, distracting the chatty receptionist. Star made her break, scooting off to the dressing room that adjoined Arena One. Once ensconced in the dressing room, Star put her belongings into one of the wood-paneled wardrobes. As she slid out of her skirt, she listened to the music and the familiar husky voice of Belinda. Of all the aerobics teachers under her supervision, Belinda had stood out from the beginning, soon becoming Star's favorite protégé. Normally, Star would've gone to her office and changed in her own private dressing room, but Deidra had held her up and she didn't want to miss the end of Belinda's class. She smiled as she heard the woman's voice instructing her students to, "Stick it out and pull it in, stick it out again, again, 'cause that's the way—uhuh, uhuh—we like it—uhuh uhuh. That's the way—uhuh, uhuh— we like it, uhuh, uhuh. Stick it out and…"

Star lingered a little longer, just listening, and then walked out onto the stage of Arena One. Belinda greeted her with a wave, incorporating this gesture into the beat. Star watched the energetic movements of the lithe Jazzercise instructor. This was one of the most popular classes, with its hit music and original choreography. Belinda really had the attention of the women. They were working hard, trying their best to give their instructor what she wanted while clearly enjoying every minute of it. Many were professional women who felt they owed it to themselves to come to a luxurious spa and work out a few times a week.

It took Star only a moment to pick up the routine. She soon began to perform the fluid, rhythmic movements in the background. The women's eyes flitted between her and Belinda as the two of them moved in unison. To them, when Star joined in, it added to the harmonious atmosphere and sophisticated operation of the club.

All too soon, the routine ended. Star felt a flicker of disappointment and tried to pinpoint it. Partly she knew she missed leading classes, feeling that high energy. But she knew it was more than not having found a way to replace that foregone high. No job, no matter how glamorous or rewarding, could fulfill a person completely. *What else do you need?* she asked herself. *The traditional husband and kids? That sure won't be happening anytime soon,* she told herself.

As Belinda gave the panting women some last minute instructions, Star wandered to the floor-length window and gazed down at the glistening, traffic-clogged street. She wondered whether she should go back to Blueberry Run tonight or to her own place—a condo in the southern Philadelphia suburb, just a fifteen-minute bus ride from the Placido.

She quickly decided to stay at the condo. It was only a few miles north of Wilmington where the support group meeting would be held the next day. Star perked up as she thought about the group and about spending the night in her own place.

She loved the condo. The multilevel two-bedroom place carried special meaning because she'd purchased it after receiving a huge bonus from one of her first big assignments. And it was her own space. She hadn't been able to spend much time there lately, though. She'd virtually moved in with Gail to help with the unpacking and Nanette. The thirty-five-mile drive from Blueberry Run to Philly certainly hadn't been a hardship, but now that Gail had pretty much settled into her new home and neighborhood, Star relished the thought of being in her own place again, at least sometimes. And maybe she needed to take a trip or start going out more. Not to meet men, as Gail constantly encouraged her to do, but just to have something different to do at night.

"Yep. Wind, rain, and traffic can really be fascinating," Belinda said, shaking Star from her thoughts.

Star turned to her, saying, "Yeah, it is totally delightful, if you know what I mean." The women chuckled.

"I see you've added a few new twists to one of my old routines," Star said, getting back to work. "I loved that move at the end."

Belinda, dark-haired, green-eyed, and reed-slender, twisted the towel that encircled her long neck. She dabbed at her forehead, which still glistening with sweat. "Well, I had to change your ending, Star. I was afraid they'd throw something out of joint. It'll be a while before they can make that hip loop."

"That's good judgment. You know what I always say, if it won't work, don't use it. It all depends on the group you're working with."

Belinda basked in the glow of Star's approval. "Did you see the look in their eyes when they were watching us? They loved it! We should do that more often."

"Yeah," Star said, "I loved it myself. I sometimes miss being an instructor. There's nothing like that surge you get when you're out front, leading the pack."

"Well, I've had enough of leading the pack for one day. Now that I'm through, I just want to go home and curl up next to my husband. If I'm lucky, he'll give me a total body workout." Belinda gave Star a wink and then headed for the staff showers.

Star finished her rounds, observing the other aerobics sessions and chatting briefly with the instructors. Done with this, she circled back to the dressing room next to Arena One and retrieved her belongings. Then she went to her office. She settled onto the taupe couch and flipped through her messages again before picking up the phone.

After she'd returned her strictly business calls, she called Rex and they firmed up their dinner plans. She'd have enough time for a long luxurious shower before meeting him at seven. She made one last call to check in with Eunice Nichols, the director of the community center in Wilmington where her support group would meet the next day. That accomplished, she headed for her private shower.

—⁓—

By 6:50 P.M., Star was sitting in the Windjammer restaurant, sipping a glass of white wine while she waited for Rex. Seven o'clock couldn't come fast enough—she was ravenous. While the Windjammer's food was considered good, the atmosphere was truly sensational, even unforgettable to some. Overlooking the bay, the restaurant rose high and majestic above the water. Inside, its three-tiered curved split-level structure allowed a panoramic view of all the goings-on. Tropical colored mobiles with seafaring themes hung from the ceiling. Thick carpeting with a matching tropical motif covered the floors on every level. Waiters and waitresses, attired in assorted hot pink and aqua outfits flitted about sporting big smiles and begging to be of help. Each level featured a huge salad bar, offering all the regular fare plus a host of rare delicacies. At least two waiters or waitresses stood at these bars to explain what each delicacy was, where it came from, and how it should be eaten.

On such a blustery night, Star hadn't expected such a huge crowd. Perhaps the many diners had deliberately chosen the Windjammer, knowing its tropical island ambiance would ward off the dreary evening outside.

She certainly was soaking up the atmosphere and anticipating the good food to follow. She took another sip of wine, peered at her watch, and turned slightly in her chair to see if Rex was approaching. Not yet, she noted, as she turned back to the table.

A man stood on the other side of the small table, but she quickly realized it wasn't Rex. Before looking up to meet this man's eyes, she prepared what she hoped would be a convincing explanation for why he couldn't join her. A moment later, she realized her preparation was insufficient, for she found herself staring into the eyes of Daran Ajero. She was startled and her mouth fell open, but only for a moment.

"Hello," his deep voice resounded as those eyes complimented her on her appearance. "I wondered for a moment if I was seeing things," he continued. "I didn't expect to see you here."

Star regained her composure. She extended her hand and held his smooth fingers briefly. But that contact and his probing eyes made her all too vividly recall their last meeting—his lips against her skin.

His head turned slowly in both directions before he asked, "Is my friend parking the car?"

For a moment, she wondered if he referred to Rex. But how could he know Rex? He meant Larry— her supposed spouse. Star felt jumpy. Apparently a double life created problems. It certainly made her tense. She knew she should tell him the truth.

"No, I'm meeting a friend here. Larry's still away," she replied, smiling politely. "What are you doing here?"

He was wearing a black-and-white hound's-tooth check suit with a white shirt and dark tie. The whiteness of the shirt made a striking contrast against the rich, burnished chocolate of his skin. The suit covered his tall muscular frame superbly, and he wore it with the ease of a man who wears suits often.

"I just returned from London last night with a client. He wanted to eat seafood, so what better place could I bring him than the Windjammer?" Daran's mouth smiled as he talked to her, but his eyes had become stormy.

As he gazed upon her oval-shaped face, framed by the short-cropped hair, he wanted to reach down and stroke her creamy skin. Her full, moist lips beckoned him. Her dark, slightly tilted eyes cautioned him, however. And damn it, she was another man's wife!

She watched him take inventory of her face while he talked. Some people looked into your eyes when they talked to you, Star thought, but his eyes moved over her every feature. She squirmed, wondering if this was just his way of looking at any person he talked to or whether this was his macho inspection of her as a woman. Whatever the case, the man had a way of shattering her usual composure.

"Where's your client?" she asked conversationally. She still felt jittery. "He'll think you've gotten lost."

"Oh, not at all. He's sitting over there." Daran nodded toward a location slightly to the left and back of Star. "He's watching me talk to you." Then almost in a whisper, he added, "He'll understand."

Star smiled but felt flutters in the pit of her stomach. *Whatever did this man mean? He spoke in riddles, and she wondered what he was thinking. He stood there, supposedly just talking to his friend's wife, but his eyes lingered on her face.* He continued to unsettle her. Maybe he knew the truth about the little act she was playing. She felt confused and couldn't exactly remember why she'd begun playing it in the first place. She needed to tell him the truth, wipe the slate clean, and start all over again.

She took a sip of her wine just to have something to do with her hands, and wondered how to begin saying, "I'm not married to Larry; I'm his sister-in-law." No, too abrupt, she thought. She would lead up to it by saying, "You're going to think I'm asylum material, but I just pretended to be Larry's wife." Or would she forthrightly say, "Since you just assumed I was married to Larry, I just let you think it was true. That'll teach you to go around assuming things about people."

"I guess the rain is delaying my friend," she said aloud.

Once more Daran's face became overcast. He looked suddenly overtaken by a more intense emotion as he stared at her. Star wondered if her confession had popped out unwittingly. She pressed her lips together tightly as she fought to control another wave of butterflies in her stomach. She noticed that he took a deep breath and the smile returned.

As he opened his mouth to say something more, she leaned slightly to one side, seeing Rex approaching behind him. Her face broke into a radiant smile displaying huge dimples, and Daran noticed small half-moon smile lines that intersected with the corners of her mouth.

He turned to greet her friend and momentarily froze. "That traffic is horrendous," the tall, square-shouldered man said as he stopped at the table and smiled down into Star's shining eyes. He stood next to Daran and the subtle scent of an expensive cologne floated through the air. "A couple of times I thought about just leaving the car and walking." He leaned down and kissed Star near her mouth.

"That wouldn't have ranked high among the most intelligent things you've done," Star chuckled as she wagged her finger at him. Then remembering her manners, she turned her face to Daran. A faint frown creased his forehead and she noticed a furrow between his thick eyebrows.

"Rex, this is one of my neighbors from Blueberry Run, Daran Aj—" She turned for Daran's help. "Say your last name, Daran."

Damn looked at Rex for a long moment. "Daran Ajero," he enunciated, ignoring Rex's hand. "I've got a client waiting," he said to Star and walked away.

His abrupt departure stunned Star. The man's attitude had taken a 180-degree turn. Before he had radiated charm and congeniality, but his rude departure left a chill in the air.

"Did I interrupt something?" Rex asked as he sat down, still watching Daran stalk off to his table.

"Nothing really," Star answered, feeling a bit disconcerted. "It's…well, nothing."

"Oh, it was something all right," Rex said, noticing her flushed face. "Hey, I'm still shivering, but—If He held up his palm to ward off further protestations.

"Remember, I'm your friend, Star. You can tell me when you get ready." He picked up the menu. "Right now I want to eat."

"Honestly, Rex, I'm not sure," she said, feeling the need to explain. But what to explain? She didn't know. Silently she steadied herself and forced her eyes to focus on the menu.

They ordered, and when the food arrived Rex ate his stuffed trout with his usual gusto, chatting all the while about the usual goings-on at the Placido.

Star merely nibbled at her sole almandine. She could feel Daran Ajero's eyes boring holes in her back. The man undoubtedly thought that since Larry was away, she was out with a boyfriend. There he went assuming again. He wasn't the guardian angel of her marriage. Darn! Star thought. Now I'm beginning to believe my own lie. But I didn't tell a lie, she reminded herself. Yeah, but you should have cleared up the misunderstanding right away, another voice pointed out. Why did you want him to think you were married? I don't know, she replied. Yes, you do. You do. You do. The voice resounded. Then, why, she demanded. It's because you like the way he looks at you, the other voice replied with a gleeful smirk. Oh, yeah, she said, I'll bet he looks at every woman like that. Ah-ha! So that's what you're afraid of—that he's a man on the make, the voice fairly screamed.

Star's lips curved into a tiny smile. Fortunately she could mask it by pretending to wipe some food from the corner of her mouth. If I keep this up, I'll end up with a split personality, she thought, and she tried to concentrate on what Rex was saying about a recent weekend spent at a Club Med resort.

Instead she found her mind wandering back to when she'd first met Rex. That was back at the Aerobics Institute during a physiology class. Since he was one of only three male students and by far the handsomest, the other women in the class catered to him. Star had never been attracted to a man simply because of his looks and Rex was no exception. She thought the other women were acting like adolescent girls. Sometimes she caught his eye across the large exercise room and he'd look at her in a puzzled way. Then one day he caught up with her as she left the building.

"Either you don't like me or I appeal to you so strongly you're scared of what can happen," he'd said.

She laughed, saying, "I'll tell you what. Let's assume we're already good friends who talk to each other about our love lives. You tell me about why you broke up with your last girlfriend."

Her direct manner shocked him at first. Then he cocked his head to one side, pursed his lips, and said, "Okay, I'll play. I'm nothing if not adventurous."

Just as she expected, he launched into a detailed physical description of the girlfriend. Tall, slender, and very pretty. He talked about the clothes she wore, where she lived and worked, her favorite music, and the places she liked to go.

When he'd finished, she repeated, "Yes, but tell me about your last girlfriend." His confusion seemed to root him to the spot. "What do you mean? I just did."

"No, you told me things about her—outside things, surface things. You didn't tell me the kind of person she was or what traits made her the kind of person she was. You didn't tell me her political views or her priorities. Her fantasies, or what hurt or disappointed her. Nothing about her happiest times, what she really loved about herself, what made her angry, or if she never got angry, why not?"

She paused then, noting that while he looked at her, he was searching through the past for some answers. He'd instinctively known she'd penalize him for a lack of answers, or worse, the wrong answers.

He answered her questions with questions, first licking those lips that seemed the work of a master sculptor. Then he regarded her with his most flattering heavy-lidded gaze and asked, "Are you seeing somebody? I'd much rather hear about you instead."

"Shame, shame," she said, laughing and rubbing one finger against the other. "But now I know how you handle conflict—you avoid it."

"Ain't that the truth," he said, and they'd both laughed. Relieved she wouldn't press him more on this subject, he quickly told her about a Middle Eastern restaurant where they served a delicious lamb goulash.

They'd gone there, and later he said he liked being with her.

She hadn't known what he meant at the time, but in the coming months, she understood that although Rex went out of his way to project and promote his macho persona, he enjoyed being with her—a woman who wasn't on the make for his manly charms. Surprisingly, he had a young daughter who lived with him, and his mother took care of the child.

Now at the Windjammer, he complained about the Placido. As he told her how he'd been having to cover for Christina, what with her obsession with her new boyfriend, Star realized how much she enjoyed having him for a friend. He was highly entertaining, possessing a quick wit and a gift for mimicry.

In the two years of their friendship, he had proposed to her several times. She never even considered saying yes. Their friendship hadn't and never would develop into a romance. Rex was simply too shallow and superficial for Star's liking. This was most evident in his refusal to tell anyone at the club about his daughter. When she occasionally came to the club with his mother, he pretended she was his sister. The child had been born of a fling with an exotic dancer, who'd put the baby up for adoption.

It was Rex's mother who had insisted he go and get his child. Star had never told him why she turned down his proposals of marriage.

She didn't want to hurt him, and besides, she didn't think he'd understand that any man she married would have to have depth and stand for something. He had to at least be aware of what made the world turn. Rex considered politics and economics supremely boring. She'd watched his opinions and beliefs change with the wind. And while she could accept fickleness and frivolousness in a friend, she could never accept it in the man who would be her mate. For all his failings, Rex was loyal and dependable, the same qualities Star sought in female friends.

When they were out together people often told them they looked perfect for each other—two perfectly physiqued, attractive people. Their co-workers at the Placido knew about Rex's devotion to Star. They couldn't understand why she wasn't interested in a man as handsome and charming as Rex. Some of the women sought her advice on how they could spark his interest in them. Star silently felt that if they wanted Rex they probably deserved him, but she would offer them no help.

The waitress pouring the coffee brought her mind back to her immediate surroundings. She shifted in her chair and turned her head slightly to see whether her rude neighbor and his client were still there.

"They're gone. They left a few minutes ago," Rex said, noticing her sly glance.

Star's eyes met his. Then she rose. "I've got to call Gail and let her know I won't be back tonight. Back in a sec."

CHAPTER 3

As Star made her call to Gail, she knew she was being watched. She replaced the receiver in its cradle, and then turned slowly to see Daran Ajero leaning against an adjacent wall. He had his arms folded across his chest and looked at her intently.

Feeling instantly jittery, Star attempted to be cordial. "So here you are again," she said, giving him what she knew was a pathetic imitation of a smile. She then began to walk past him and away

But he said, "Next you'll tell me I'm just the person you expected to run into here tonight, aside from your male friend." He virtually spat this last word. His tone of voice, its unfamiliar biting quality, stopped her just as she came abreast of him. She turned to face him, but he looked past her, directing his gaze on some distant point rather than look at her directly.

Star's heart raced. The recessed lights shone on his smooth dark skin.

His breathing was fast and his nostrils flared. She knew the man was fuming mad. His heightened emotions only intensified his raw masculine energy. A dizzying wave washed over Star. She became woozy and began to perspire. He's undoubtedly an appealing man, but meddling is such a turnoff, she thought, trying to recover herself.

She bolstered herself and said, "Now, really, Daran, or should I say, Mr. Ajero, it's time for you to know something. I'm not—"

"You're not cheating on your husband, you're just out with an old friend who can't keep his hands off you." His eyes riveted hers now. Even the dim lighting could not conceal the fury in those usually smiling eyes.

"I am out with a friend and I'm not cheating on my husband, and it's not your damn business anyway." Star spoke through clenched teeth, trying to steel her nerves.

With one fluid movement, he came so close to her that the heat from his body pummeled hers. His nostrils flared as he stared down into her face. And despite her anger at him, his virility hit her with another dizzying wave.

"I don't need you to tell me what's my business," he growled. "You women act so modest and innocent, but you're really just schemers—just waiting for the man to get barely out of sight before you're out with your friends."

His accusation infuriated her, and the sheer audacity of the man was unsurpassed. He was a meddler, always butting in, just like at the supermarket. No matter what, she would stand her ground and let him make an utter fool of himself. She struggled to control both her tongue and her expression and succeeded in smiling placidly at him.

"Is that all? I wouldn't dare miss the rest of your lecture, but I do want to get back to my friend."

Her calm manner and words of polite dismissal apparently fueled his anger. "Larry is my friend, but even if he weren't, I want you to know that decent married women don't consort with male friends. Only sl—"

"Excuse me! But who died and made you king?" Star was appalled by her corny retort, but for now, it was the best she could do. Whatever the words, she had to make this arrogant meddler know that what she did was none of his business. All politeness had left her. She aimed and through clenched teeth, let him have it with her parting shot. "Besides, I'm not even Larry's wife!"

His eyes went wide. She could almost hear his wheels whirring and spinning as her words sank in. She had finally punctured his big balloon of supreme self-assurance. Flashing him a smile of sheer satisfaction, Star spun on her heels and strolled away. The old saying should have been "*She* who laughs last, laughs best," she thought as she walked triumphantly away.

Star stayed silent for most of the half-hour drive from the Windjammer to the condo. When Rex asked if he could come inside, she claimed she was tired. There were times when she just had to be absolutely alone, and this was one of them.

Tempestuous emotions raged in her and she needed to know why. Granted the events of the evening had been extremely unsettling, but she had encountered arrogant people numerous times in the course of her work and had dealt with them in the appropriate way. What was the appropriate way in this case? The question itself was murky and the answer seemed piled under layers of obscurity. She had no intention of wading through all that tonight.

As she mounted the spiral stair to the third level of the condo, her mind kept replaying the events of the evening: Daran Ajero's surprising appearance at the restaurant, his words to her, the timbre of his deep voice, the nuances of his words, and the way he looked at her with those striking eyes. And then his accusations coupled with the memory of his lips touching her skin that day on the porch. The feeling of that moment shot through her now. Even now, her legs wobbled so that she had to grasp the stair's railing for support.

Undoubtedly, he was a very attractive man, but he was far too imperious and chauvinistic for her taste. Being an African, he'd probably insist that his woman be barefoot and pregnant and walk two steps behind him at all times. Look at the way he treated her—like she belonged to Larry. He probably felt it was his responsibility as a man to help keep her in line while her man was away.

But safely in her bedroom, as Star peeled off each item of her clothing, she wondered what Daran would say if he could see her now. She imagined his eyes crawling over each part of her body.

Just before she pulled her short nightie over her head, she paused and gazed in the mirror at her lithe, slender frame, her small, full breasts. Her eyes moved down to her flat stomach, then past the dark, curly triangle to the spot where his lips had seared the soft flesh of her inner thigh. She squirmed and her nipples tingled. The image of Daran Ajero leapt before her, but his eyes did not contain their usual amusement. Instead, they were languid but fervent, pausing longer in some places, pausing forever before he touched.

Star shivered. She clenched her eyes, teeth, and hands tightly, trying to blot out his image. She succeeded in calling up the memory of his contorted features as he had lashed out at her in the restaurant—as if she were an immoral child. The memory reminded her of her indignation at his patronizing attitude—feelings she was too tired to relive right now.

She dove into bed. As soon as her head hit the pillow, all the day's events took their toll, and moments later she fell soundly asleep.

Driving south on Interstate 95 the next morning, Star felt like a new person. Cool, crisp air blew through the Mazda Miata's open windows, invigorating her, while the sun's steady rays gave her a great feeling of well-being. So did her anticipation of the first women's support group meeting.

She pulled into the parking lot of Wilmington's Crane Community Center at exactly ten-fifteen. When she'd spoken to Eunice Nichols yesterday, she'd promised she'd be in early to help set up for the eleven o'clock meeting.

She took a few moments and found herself reflecting on how things just seemed to happen right sometimes. She'd met Eunice at a workshop on women's health issues at the College of Delaware. The two had hit it off, and when Star told her about her idea for a black women's support group that focused on the emotional side of health, Eunice had offered her support and the use of the Crane Center. "I know just what you mean," Eunice had said then. "A woman can get very frustrated when all her life is about being everything to everybody, and all the while she's neglecting herself. If she's lucky, the kids may sometimes say 'Thanks, Mom' and if there's a man in her life, he might say 'Thanks, honey.'

"And there may be those superficial displays on her birthday or on Mother's Day. But does anyone ever look a woman in the eye and ask: Who are you? What are your needs? What do you need from me? How can I help you get what you really need?"

Star had laughed. "And most likely, the woman wouldn't be able to answer the questions because she doesn't know herself. That's why a support group is so important. It'll be a place for the woman to focus on herself. Three hours each month just for her. And it'll help her think about her needs during the time between meetings. It'll be a place where a woman can focus on her needs and the stressors in her life in the presence of other women who care about her and share many of her experiences. This group will be really uplifting and empowering, because we women will see that we know what we need and can find ways to solve our problems together."

Star and Eunice had chattered on, hungrily almost. Both of them were so happy to have found someone else who shared her ideas, a kindred spirit.

With these warm memories, Star crossed the parking lot to the center's entrance. Once inside, she got right to work.

As today was the first meeting and Star knew the importance that first impression would make, she concentrated on making the center's women's lounge look as inviting as possible. Thankfully, someone had sewn some cheery curtains and made matching slipcovers for the comfortable chairs and couches. These bright colors, coupled with the sunshine streaming through the window and the smell of the coffee perking, set just the tone Star wanted.

Hooray, she thought to herself. The day has finally come.

From the very first time she read the proposal Eunice had shown her for the Women's Support and Health Network—the national group she now hoped to form a local chapter of—she'd been intrigued by how the whole idea of women coming together in small groups to appreciate and support each other could serve as the extended family that some no longer had.

Star had realized years ago that exercise and dieting were not enough to maintain good health; stress and unmet needs could undermine the best exercise and diet programs. Dieting could get the weight off, but by itself could not keep the weight off. After all, what good was it being physically fit if the emotions were being neglected? A woman needed more than a physically fit body. Good emotional health was the missing piece of the puzzle.

Seeing the need for a place to address emotional issues, and an alternative to going the

route of the psychiatrist's couch had sparked her to
set up such a group. But she'd come to recognize
she was also motivated by the need to have an
extended family of sorts. She and Gail sorely
missed "the folks" and the small-town atmosphere
of Gaiterville, where they'd been raised.

When she lived in New York, she attended a
couple of group meetings where skilled group
leaders deftly helped women lift the superficial
cloak of correct behavior that women show the
public. Once these women contacted the core of
their essence and felt the pain of their muffled
needs, they cried, screamed, and raged in a safe
place-amongst others who shared many of their
experiences and pain. By shattering this conspiracy
of silence and facing the problem squarely, solu-
tions became simpler.

Star remembered those meetings now as she
tossed some of the huge throw pillows on the floor
near the comfortable couch. She wanted the
women to feel completely at home and to sit on the
carpeted floor if they wanted. It was also necessary
for them to sit near each other.

She had just finished arranging the seating area
and distributing snacks on paper plates when she
heard footsteps on the tiled hallway outside the

lounge. The footsteps stopped and Star looked toward the lounge's double doors. She saw a small, fortyish woman standing there reading the announcement for the meeting that was posted outside the door.

"If you're looking for the women's health network meeting, you've found it," Star said, smiling. She held out her hands in a welcoming gesture, and said, "Come on in. I'm Star."

As she drove to Blueberry Run that evening, Star reflected on the events of the past few hours. Things had gone well. Eight women in all had shown up. After the coffee and Danish, the women had sat back waiting to hear about the philosophy and practices of the health network.

"It's simple," Star had told them, sitting among them in the circle. "Good health involves paying as much attention to your emotional state as you do to calories, cholesterol, and fat intake. You go to the doctor for one and you come here for the other. Here, in the midst of friends, we can share our feelings and experiences. Hopefully, we'll be like family one day. It will take time for some of you to trust, but once you've reached that point, the benefits will be great. You'll find out along the way that we are not here to judge you; we're here to support you and help you reach your goal of all-around health. We're all here for the same reason."

After this introduction, all the women warmed up. They said it was about time for such a group and asked questions about how often the meetings would be, how long they would last, what form the meetings would take, and so on.

"What do you think?" Star asked them, waving her hand to include all of them. "We're all in charge."

In no time, the structural details of the group were ironed out.

Toward the end of the three hours, Star held up the thick manual she'd received from Eunice. It contained the guiding philosophy of the Women's Support and Health Network and guidelines for establishing a local chapter.

"I don't know all the answers," she said as her eyes sought and met the eyes of each of the women there, "but we all know that it's time we took our emotional health into our own hands. We haven't done it before because we're blind in a way. So, ladies, this manual"—she held it out to them—"will be our Seeing Eye dog, and I will make everyone of you a copy of it."

"Yeah, and I'm gonna read that sucker to make sure it can see," said Janice, a short, round woman who exuded warmth and congeniality.

All the women had laughed and the official meeting broke up, but it was another hour before any of them left. After making plans for the next meeting, they munched and talked, and munched and talked some more.

Star felt tremendously buoyed. Already this coming together was improving the quality of their lives—of her life. And Gail had promised to join once the group had a firm footing.

When she left the center, she felt like she was bouncing. She headed for the fish market, and after buying some shrimp and some of the farm-raised fresh catfish Gail loved, she drove to Blueberry Run satisfied that the day had gone perfectly. It wasn't often a person was able to see an idea come to life.

As she turned into the development, a black pickup truck zoomed toward her. Instinctively, Star swerved, just missing the truck. It barely slowed before roaring on out, but Star caught a glimpse of the woman behind the wheel. Star quickly recalled the face. It was the same woman who had come to get Daran Ajero two weeks before.

Star looked back to see the pickup waiting to turn onto the main highway not more than a few yards away. The driver seemed unaware she'd nearly run Star off the road. The woman sat there, eyes forward, her head at a haughty angle.

Star was almost amused by her. She thought that at times like these a man would no doubt swear about "women drivers." She wondered what men said about lousy male drivers. Probably they'd just be called lousy drivers, with no gender attached.

Anyway, nothing, not even a near collision, could dampen her spirits this afternoon. This was a day she'd accomplished something big—something she'd wanted for a long time. Even as a child, Star knew she wanted to help people. She felt like she'd come full circle.

She turned into the driveway but didn't see Gail's Olds coupe. Star parked her car and walked the short distance to the front door. She felt disappointed that she would have to wait to tell Gail about the success of the first meeting.

Gail must have gone out to catch a sale because that would be the only reason she'd leave the house on a Saturday, Star thought. Gail hated her forty mile workday commute so much that she arranged all her shopping and running errands so she wouldn't have to drive anywhere on weekends.

While fishing through her gigantic leather purse for the house key, Star heard Gail's voice coming from the house. Surprised, she peered through the filmy curtains that covered the windows flanking the front door and caught a glimpse of Gail walking from the dining room into the kitchen. Star rang the doorbell.

She saw Gail look at her quizzically before she broke into her familiar, beaming smile. She opened the door, saying, "Girl, I thought you were a salesman or some of those church folks who come around. Why didn't you use your key?"

"Where's your car?" Star queried. "When I didn't see your car, I thought you'd gone out. Is something wrong?"

"Of course not. My car is in the garage. Come on in here. I have to feed Nan." Gail led the way through the large foyer toward the kitchen. "I do park the car in the garage sometimes. You just probably never noticed." Then peering at Star's face, Gail asked, "What's up?"

"I was just anxious to tell you how well the meeting went, and when I didn't see your car right away, I thought I'd have to wait. You know how I like to spill it out—good or bad."

"Well, good. The group went well, but now that I know that much, I'll wait for the details. But do I have something to tell you! You gonna hafta kick off your shoes and get comfortable for this, chile."

Gail always reverted to their southern dialect when she had some especially juicy gossip to relate. From the look on her face, Star knew Gail could barely contain herself. She smiled, recalling how as girls they'd sworn they'd never be reduced to gossiping like Aunt Mellie and her old friends.

Star followed her sister's angular physique to the kitchen. She knew she'd have to wait for Gail to have her say about whatever had happened before she could tell her anything more about the group. Maybe a neighboring couple had had a fight and the wife had come to Gail for help. Since the houses were all at least two acres apart, Gail certainly couldn't have overheard anything and could see precious little.

Star put the fish she had bought into the refrigerator, poured herself a glass of apple juice, and sat down at the table in the kitchen dining nook. "All ready. What's going on?"

Gail needed no further urging. "Helena called this morning. Guess whose marriage is already on the rocks?" Gail's eyes sparkled with the anticipation of Star's reaction to her news.

"Whose? Helena's?"

"No, Lance's!" Gail punctuated her words with an exaggerated nod.

"I don't believe it."

"You'd better, 'cause Helena said that his wife left him and moved back to her parents' home—with the baby," Gail said, pursing her lips and nodding her head again to emphasize this last point.

"Did Helena say what happened—you know, the details?"

"Something about another woman." The words dripped from Gail's lips and her bright, expressive eyes met Star's dark ones.

Suddenly needing some support to digest this news, Star leaned on the kitchen island counter and stared out of one of the large windows. She couldn't really see anything, though. Instead she found herself remembering the night she'd found out Lance was to marry another girl—one from a nearby town. Feelings of humiliation and betrayal flooded her as they did each time she remembered this—the way their two-year relationship had ended. If he'd had the decency to come to her and talk about it, she wouldn't have felt so stupid and used. But no, he had sought the easiest way out. Never mind if it made her the object of people's pity. Never mind if it would make her forever mistrust her own feelings and her ability to judge men.

When the news of Lance's impending marriage had begun to spread through the grapevine, Star had felt as if she were the last to know. She hadn't seen him for three weeks. After they'd had one of their all-too-frequent fights, he'd gone off. But this had happened before, and although Star had known their relationship was on the decline, if not dead, she'd never expected it would end with her hearing about his marrying another girl. Just like that, without a word to her.

She walked around in a stupor for weeks afterwards, wondering how he could have treated her so shabbily. She wondered how she could have been so blind and trusting. Gail had warned her that Lance wasn't right for her.

"Star, he's insensitive, selfish, and he struts around like he's God's gift to you. I would give him his walking papers in a hurry."

Star had chalked it up to a personality clash between them. After all, Gail was the type to take an instant dislike to people. Lance had been attentive at times. Constantly he'd told her how perfect she was for him. And he'd been her first and only sexual experience.

She shuddered and Gail came over and hugged her. "Just let it go, Star. That was three years ago and a long ways away. You've got to know that marrying Lance would've wrecked your life. Consider yourself lucky. Imagine how his little wife feels. She married him in haste and now she will have lots of time to repent in leisure, whether they get back together or not."

"I know, Gail," Star said, forcing a smile. It's just I hadn't given that whole episode more than a passing thought in a while. I know I'm lucky. I just don't feel like it sometimes."

Just then Star noticed the open cookbooks. Gail never used cookbooks unless company was coming. She gave her sister a puzzled look. "You didn't say you were having company."

"We're having company, sister dear," she said, smiling, a devilish gleam in her eye.

When the doorbell rang, Star's stomach almost leapt out of her body. She felt panic tinged with a rippling excitement surging through every part of her being. She stood there hoping Gail would come quickly and open the door. Quite irrationally, she left the family room and almost raced to the adjoining kitchen, where she busied herself feverishly cleaning off the counter. She didn't understand the intensity of the anxiety that washed over her body in wave after wave. She only knew she was in the grips of something she could barely contain or control.

When the doorbell rang a second time, she stood rooted at the kitchen sink, meticulously cleaning the drain basket.

"Get that, will you, Star?" came Gail's voice through the intercom. "I'm changing Nan and maybe I can get her to sleep then. Tell Daran I'll be down soon."

Star forced herself to move slowly toward the front door, willing her usual composure to return.

Glancing through the left window, she saw the slender muscular form of Daran Ajero dressed in a tan, short-sleeved safari jacket and matching slacks. His white shirt was open at the neck to reveal a striking contrast of hairless dark brown skin.

Taking a deep breath, she opened the door. Neither of them spoke for a long moment. He broke the silence.

"Are you going to let me in?" His soft voice had a teasing quality and his berry-brown eyes flickered with a strange light.

Star shivered slightly. "Oh, sure, come on in." She stood aside as he entered the spacious foyer.

She moved toward the living room with him in tow. "Have a seat," she said, directing him to the bright floral love seat across from a matching sofa. "Gail is busy with the baby. She'll be down in a few minutes."

"Will she?" he said, moving closer to where she stood.

He relished her. He wanted to stand as close to her as he could. All of the known senses and some he never knew he had came alive and stood at full attention around her. He stood so close that the top of her natural hairstyle, cropped in a stylish asymmetrical cut, almost touched his nose. The fruity smell of her shampoo and her other delightful scents assailed him. A quake erupted in his loins. When she looked up at him, he noticed the quizzical expression of her large, dark eyes. As determined as he was to remain composed, the creamy, smooth texture of her skin and her moist, open, full lips did crazy things to him. His hands began to twitch. He quickly shoved them into his pockets.

Jolted by the turbulence in his eyes, Star trembled slightly and strode across the living room, away from him. "Why don't you sit down and get comfortable?" she asked again, pausing at the end of the long sofa.

Daran's eyes traveled lazily from her face, moving down her angular but very female form. The light from a desk lamp danced on her bare caramel legs, extending gracefully down from a slim knee-length skirt that hugged her curves. He shifted uncomfortably.

"We have to" —he swallowed—"talk." His eyes had moved to her long, slim feet, which were sheathed in white jeweled moccasins. He studied the stitching of her shoes to divert his attention from other parts of her.

"No, we don't, and you don't have to apologize," she said, moving to the wet bar that sat conveniently in a corner adjoining the dining room. "Would you like a beer?"

He sauntered across the living room toward her, his discomfort of just a few minutes before now replaced by seeming nonchalance.

"I'm not about to apologize. I'm not the one who pretended to be married. Do you make it a practice of pretending to be married when you meet a man?"

As he spoke, Daran's mind dipped into the past, remembering Elaine, who had seemed to be the perfect woman for him until he finally saw her true colors. Were any of these women what they seemed to be? Were all of them driven by demons that leaped out unexpectedly to play havoc with a man's dreams?

He shook his head. He wasn't thinking sensibly. He barely knew this woman and here he was comparing her with Elaine. Sure he had his hopes, for a woman like Star made any man hope to spend some very pleasurable hours with her and he hadn't been with a woman for a while now. Since Elaine, all desire for female companionship had been fleeting and manageable. Until now. Until Star.

No matter how alluring she was, he decided right then to take it slow with this woman. He could only hope his body, suddenly ravenous for the touch of a woman, would cooperate.

Star busied herself, getting the beer from the wet bar's small, built-in refrigerator and then taking the top off the bottle.

Daran watched her bite her full bottom lip before she finally answered him.

"Let's set the record straight here. I never said I was married. You just assumed it. Just like you assumed I wasn't in line at the supermarket. And just like you assumed that I was cheating on my husband." She paused. "You do a lot of assuming, and I just wanted to teach you a lesson." She smiled.

He chuckled. "So now that you've taught me a lesson, let's start all over. I'm Daran Ajero, and I'd like to get to know you—the real you," he said.

Star poured the cold beer into a glass and pressed it into his outstretched hand. "How many years do you have?" she bantered.

"Whoops, a real complicated woman," he remarked smiling. "You sound like an adventure."

"No, just multidimensional."

"If I'm going to learn about your dimensions, we'll have to go out sometime soon, like tonight." His voice was soft and teasing, but his eyes were watchful.

Smiling, she sighed and brought her hands up and pressed her hair flat, but no sooner had she removed her hands than her thick dark hair sprang up again.

"Let's just be neighbors. You know, those people who live in the same neighborhood. Who smile and wave and get together in a neighborly way sometimes. Let's do that." She took a coaster from the shelf and extended it to him. "Now go over there and sit down on that chair before Gail tells me I've forgotten about that ole time southern hospitality."

Placing the glass of beer on the bar's countertop, he reached out as if to take the coaster but instead gently took her wrist. He slowly slid his fingers into her soft palm.

Star tried, but not hard, to pull her hand away. He held it firmly. She felt a little silly standing in the living room with a man holding her hand, but she didn't want to make a big deal out of it.

"When you finish holding my hand, I've got to use it for something," she said impatiently.

But instead of retreating, he traced her jaw line slowly with his fingertip. As it neared her chin, her lips reflexively fell apart. All the while his eyes bored into hers, amazed and tantalized at the emotions he saw there.

Star did not flinch. She could tell by the amused light in his sparkling eyes that he'd issued her a challenge. She would meet it if it was the last thing she did.

He smiled. "Now that we're on neighborly terms, why didn't you tell me you weren't married to Larry that first day in the doorway?"

She yanked her hand from his. "I told you why." He gave her a disbelieving scowl, then chuckled and shook his head.

"No, I'll tell you why." His voice had fallen several octaves and each word rang like a bell as he continued. "Something happened between us that day I came here. We both felt it, Starmaine, but you were so scared by what you felt that you had to find a way to hide. So you lied to me." He picked up the glass of beer and took a sip.

Star stood there listening to his words, enthralled by the sound of his deep voice and the way his eyes moved over her face as he talked.

"It's very simple, Star. I'm a man and you're a woman and what we feel is basic and natural. Sooner or later, we all have to answer the call of nature."

The utter gall of the man was more than Star could endure. She let out a laugh she hoped sounded convincing.

"You're just the cockiest male that I've ever met. But you're good, though. I'll give you that mueh. I'll bet you pride yourself on how many women you can talk into the sack." Her eyes locked with his. "There's nothing going on between us, Daran. Nothing. We're neighbors and we have a friendly connection through Larry. Let's leave it at that." She stopped talking but refused to let her eyes release his. Whether she meant what she said or not, she wanted to make sure that he understood how things had to be.

A second later, she realized he hadn't understood at all. It happened so fast. One moment, she was laying out the boundaries of their relationship and the next he had enveloped her in his arms. While his mouth and tongue drew at her lips and tongue, Starmaine breathed in his woodsy cologne and felt the faint stubble of his beard. Funny, his skin always looked so smooth, she hadn't even realized he shaved.

Momentarily lost in the touch of his skin, her body seemed to have a will of its own. Her arms swooped up and encircled his neck. Clad as she was in a cotton knit outfit, she felt his heart pumping against her chest. Farther down, she felt more evidence of the effect her body had on his. She reflexively responded to his urgency for an endless moment before he grasped her shoulders and held her away. His eyes scanned her face as he struggled to control his breathing. She sensed he was waiting for her to set a new course for their relationship. There was no point in denying that she had enjoyed the exchange, but that didn't mean that it would happen again.

"You're a terrific kisser," she exclaimed. "I'll bet you've had plenty of practice."

He paused and smiled. "No, it comes naturally when I'm with the right person."

"You're also very charming. I would recommend you highly in both the technique and charm categories to anyone who's interested." Star's eyes met his to see whether her casual remarks on the encounter conveyed the message she intended.

Hearing Gail's footsteps on the stairs, he moved close to her and whispered, "That's your brain talking now. But it wasn't your brain in motion a few minutes ago. And it wasn't your brain that scared you the other day, was it?" He gave her a knowing look and with a smile turned to greet her sister.

With Gail in the room, the tension was lighter but far from gone. Daran's words kept running slowly through her mind, and each glance at him told her he knew her thoughts.

Gail made them all frothy mixed drinks and brought out hot hors d'oeuvres. They all sat down and Daran and Gail chatted mainly about the difference between living in a big urban area and the sleepy little town of Blueberry Run. Whenever Daran directed a comment to Star, she tried to determine if there was an innuendo hidden in his words. And when Gail wasn't looking, Daran's vibrant brown eyes looked at her boldly.

Gail had instantly picked up the undercurrents and when Star announced she was exhausted, adding that she hadn't slept much the night before, Gail told her to go on up to bed. "I'll entertain Daran," she said. "Besides, since he's a neighbor and Larry's friend, you'll see plenty of him."

Star's comment about not sleeping had piqued Daran's interest. He looked at her intently, as if he could peer into her mind to determine the previous night's ending.

She could tell what he was wondering and wanted to yell at him that she hadn't ended the night in Rex's bed and never would, for that matter. She knew an outburst would please him to no end. She wasn't about to give him the satisfaction.

She felt his eyes on her as she walked across the living room and up the stairs. Relief washed over her when she was finally out of his sight. Silently she mouthed a string of curses that would have amazed a New York City cabdriver.

Safely upstairs, she picked up a section of the needlework she and Gail both loved to work on. Instantly she felt some of the tension ebb from her body as her fingers nimbly moved the needle through the fabric. She had not realized until that moment that her body was so taut. Talk about being stressed out!

She had to admit that the man had a knack for intruding on her life and her mind. He even had her body responding to his in a way she wouldn't soon forget. Was any part of her off-limits to him?

As she punched the needle through the thick fabric, she made a staunch vow to be in control around him in the future. Controlling and directing others was something she excelled at—at least at work. It was just a matter of adopting a certain mindset. That was how she had managed to advance in her line of work. It was an act, a kind of game.

Whatever Daran Ajero could dish out, she would counter it, or even one-up him. It would be fun. He was certainly a worthy opponent. She knew she had to be extremely careful, however, because this opponent could read her like a book. That certainly could be dangerous!

CHAPTER 4

Starmaine awoke early the next morning after a fitful sleep. The sunshine sliding through the miniblinds told her it was nearly eight o'clock. Growing up on a farm had taught her how to tell time by the position of the sun and a glance at the clock on the headboard proved her right.

It was a morning made for being outdoors, but then she loved being outside and morning had always been her favorite time of day. Things were quiet and calm then and the day brimmed with potential.

Thinking of her fantasy of the perfect morning room she'd one day have in her own home, Star donned some shorts and a lightweight sweatshirt and went downstairs to search the mud room's closet for her walking sneakers. She was careful not to make any noise. She didn't want to risk waking her little niece. Nanette would naturally wake up her mom, and Gail would feel cheated out of her Sunday morning sleep.

Moments later, Star was outside, walking down the drive to the road. There she hesitated briefly. She was not sure what route she should take for her morning walk. After all, now she was all too aware of who lived in the grand residence at the tip of the spoon-shaped road. Would he be outside this early? Did he know she walked past his house sometimes? Had he ever peeked at her as she went by? Probably not, or he'd have mentioned it.

She scolded herself for not putting on a little makeup. Just as quickly, she scoffed at the idea of putting on makeup for a workout. What would he think if he happened to be outside and saw her walking past his house wearing makeup?

Especially after she'd gone overboard last night to show him she wasn't interested in him. Not that her rebuffs had squelched him any. She recalled with detail the close attention he gave to her every movement and expression; his words and the way his eyes invaded her whenever they were alone lingered in her mind. These thoughts left her wrestling a strong and uncharacteristic bout of indecision.

Then her adventurous nature took over. *Damn him!* she thought. *I'm not going to change anything for him. He's just a man like any other man. Most likely he's asleep, and besides, he's seen me without makeup before.*

It felt invigorating to be outside. Buoyed by the cool morning air and the stillness of the outdoors, Star started off at a brisk pace, forcing herself to concentrate on the beautiful landscaping of some of the homes along the way. She recalled Gail saying Larry planned to do some plantings when he returned. Some of the other neighbors did their own landscaping; she knew because she'd seen them preparing the ground and putting in flowers and shrubs. Now that it was fall, many of the front yards were bedecked with assorted clusters of chrysanthemums, or "mums" as they were called. Star felt their brilliantly vivid yellow, purple, pink, burnt orange, or white blossoms greeted passersby with a strong statement and gave the day a cheerful cast.

She smiled and continued along the oval-shaped path that went past the house at the tip of the spoon. She steeled herself, ready to meet its occupant if she must.

As she neared Daran Ajero's house, however, she saw a figure on the long front veranda. She could tell it was not Daran. Whoever it was was too short and had totally different body movements.

Each step nearer the house made it clear that it was not a man's figure but a woman's. Starmaine remembered the day two weeks prior when the woman had come to get Daran for an important phone call. But why was the woman here at this early hour, and on a Sunday morning? Was this woman a relative of his? Or what?

A sinking feeling in Starmaine's stomach gripped her tightly and threatened to make her drop her eyes to the pavement. She wanted to scream at herself for her naiveté regarding the man, for not suspecting he had something hidden—a woman, of course. She became annoyed and simultaneously felt a pinprick of disappointment she wasn't quite able to shrug off. You're a dope, Starmaine, she told herself. How many times do you have to be hit with a raised club before you realize that a raised club will hit you? You should know by now or at least suspect that any man, especially if he's as virile, charming, and eligible as Daran Ajero, will have a woman waiting in the wings somewhere. Yet another part of her screamed: Do they all have to be the same way?

As she neared his property line, she saw the woman had moved to sit in a porch swing, hanging from the rafters at a corner of the wraparound veranda. Starmaine could feel the woman's eyes on her.

She seems to be quite at home, Starmaine thought. Well, if Starmaine was honest with herself, she couldn't see a dynamic man like Daran practicing abstinence for long.

Just as she came abreast of the house, the woman called out to her in a voice that was melodious and cheerful.

"Good morning. You are certainly working your body hard."

Starmaine slowed her pace and looked toward the house. She smiled and raised her arm to wave, but the woman was standing now and beckoning her to come up to the house.

Starmaine paused, her mind working swiftly. She couldn't very well ignore her. Besides, she was curious about this woman who sat on his porch at this early hour. She walked up the wide brick path to the house.

—⁂—

Ten minutes later, Starmaine still sat opposite the charming girlish-looking woman with the lilting voice who'd insisted Star call her Cordy, as all her friends back home did.

"Nobody calls me Cordelia but my daddy and Daran," Cordy said, with a glint of humor in her round, dark eyes. "They're always formal and serious." A slight frown creased her brow before she continued.

"My daddy's coming over here next summer for my graduation, or so he says."

Cordy clapped her hands together and her eyes sparkled. Then she leaned forward and conspiratorially lowered her voice. "By then I intend to have something definite to tell him or maybe even before then if my plan goes according to schedule."

Star sat staring at this young woman who couldn't have been more than eighteen. She possessed a vibrancy, a touch of the dramatic, and a self-assurance that made her highly interesting—no, entertaining, Star concluded.

Cordy was long-limbed, slender, and buxom. Her small, perfectly shaped head sat perched on a long slender neck. Her small, round nose between high, prominent cheekbones, combined with her full lips, gave a voluptuous cast to her animated face. Her dark skin was satiny smooth and highlighted by a natural but barely perceptible sheen. When she walked, she seemed to glide and whether she moved her head or her arms, every movement was fluid and graceful.

Fascinated by this vibrant, lithe young woman, Star sat sipping the freshly squeezed orange juice Cordy had hurriedly prepared on a rolling cart that sat nearby. "I wanted to be a model when I was in high school, but my daddy says models are prostitutes." With this, Cordy clasped her hands and brought them to her mouth. "So I decided to become a microbiologist. I'll get a double master's degree in microbiology and immunology next June."

"How old are you, anyway?" The question just popped out of Star's mouth. It was amazing that this girl or woman who barely seemed a teenager was finishing graduate school!

"Let me get you some more juice," she said, picking up Star's empty glass. "I'm thirty-one. I know I don't look it. You should see my mama, though. She looks about my age." She smiled, showing beautiful teeth. "All of the women from the Beodun area of my country stay looking young for a long time. It's been going on in our area for centuries. We are known throughout the country for that."

Though extremely comfortable in the rattan chair and enjoying herself, Star finished the orange juice and rose. "It was nice meeting and chatting with you, Cordy, but I'd better finish my walk before I just decide to sit here all day."

"That would be great because I do get lonely out here surrounded by all of this farmland with no one to talk to. Daran is always too busy." A slight frown creased the polished smoothness of her forehead again, but it disappeared just as quickly.

"Anyway, now that we've met, we can visit with each other and do things together. I'll show you how to make some of our delicious African stews and you can teach me how to make some American foods. Just bring the baby over with you." A puzzled look came over her features. "Where is the baby this morning?"

"My sister's home today, so they're both sleeping late."

"Oh, I didn't know your sister lived with you. That's just like at home. Women in Nigeria usually have their younger sister or cousin live with them to help with the children and the housework."

Before Star could explain that it was she who lived with Gail, at least part of the time, and that she was the younger sister helping out, Cordy continued. "Daran will really like it if I can make some American dishes. His clients will think that the food is very exotic."

Hearing his name again, Star became hungry for some answers and delayed her departure. She wondered where he was and concluded that he was sleeping late.

"Oh, so he doesn't like to talk?" Star inquired, picking up the thread of what Cordy had said moments ago. She remembered vividly his low, deep voice talking, almost whispering to her as his eyes crawled over her.

Cordy sighed and twisted her mouth. "Oh, he talks enough when his clients are around and he talks to me about this and that, but he won't talk to me about important things.

Star wondered what was important to this woman who was her counterpart in some ways. Cordy was only three years older than she was. They had both gone to college, though she hadn't gone to graduate school like Cordy. They had both departed from the ways of women in their cultures: Cordy by leaving her country and coming to a far land and she by working in a "glamour" job, one that few black women ever get the chance to enter.

"Well, that's the way some men are. They think our female brains are just unequipped for things other than cooking, cleaning, and having babies," Star said in her best imitation of a male chauvinist.

"That is usually the case, but Daran is very enlightened in many ways. He just treats me like this because he knew me when I was one of the small girls he'd see playing around our house when he came to visit my brother, Cheghum." Cordy frowned and her irritation was evident. "And he refuses to see me in any other way. When he comes back, I'm not going to—"

"Oh, is he away?" Star blurted. "Yes, he left early this morning to take Mr. Akimaba to the embassy in Washington."

Relieved that Daran wasn't somewhere inside the house listening to them or thinking she'd come by out of curiosity about him, Star relaxed. She sat back in the chair, while Cordy began to really talk.

When Star left Daran's house an hour later, she was in a daze from the things Cordy had told her. It had sapped all the will to walk from her body. She had to force herself to maintain an even pace. Her head buzzed with the details of Cordy's bizarre plan to marry Daran. And Cordy had pleaded with her to help her with the plan.

That's what you get for being neighborly, she chided herself. But she had to admit she'd stopped by because she was curious about the woman at Daran Ajero's house because he interested her. It was only natural that she'd want to know about a woman who shared his house. And his bed?

"I had to check out the competition," she pointed out candidly to herself, "or see if there was any. And I got all my questions answered, and then some."

She marveled at the ambitious—no, devious—plan Cordy had outlined to become Mrs. Daran Ajero.

Cordy said, "He wants me to move out of the house now because he knows my family will soon find out he's divorced and we are living together alone in this house. If my plan works out, I won't ever have to leave here because I'll have a little Daran junior well on the way by next year when my daddy comes. Then Daran will marry me—he won't have a choice. After all, our families have always known each other and we already care deeply about each other."

Star had listened to all of this, amazed. From what Cordy had implied, Star was sure that Daran was already sleeping with the woman. Scenes of intertwined limbs, damp skin, and deep guttural moans filled her mind. She imagined he would be a skilled and tireless lover, one who could make a woman weep with ecstasy.

Hearing Cordy talk about Daran and her plans for their future had caused a growing anxiety in Star. Finally she'd blurted, "But how do I fit into this? I don't know why you think I can do something to make him marry you."

It was then that Cordy had explained to her that since she was Larry's wife and since Daran thought very highly of Larry, they could be very strong allies. "I know he was over there last night and came back whistling. He respects your husband highly and obviously enjoys the friendship. He even told me he persuaded your husband to come here to buy the land and build his house. He wouldn't have done that if he did not hold him in very high esteem."

Star had felt suddenly stretched to a point she rarely reached. She smiled to soften the edge of her words as she said, "You and Daran certainly have something in common—you both assume a lot. He thought exactly the same as you." Star measured her words carefully. "But you see, I'm not Larry's wife. I'm his sister-in-law."

Cordy's forehead creased. "Sister-in-law?" She grabbed a handful of her thick dark hair as her eyes searched Star's face, looking for the answer to the puzzle. "But you just said that the baby…" She paused, struggling to make sense out of the jigsaw.

Star smiled again. "Look, Cordy, it's very simple. My sister, Gail, is Larry's wife—I'm not. I stay with my sister a lot to help out with her baby and to keep Gail company since Larry's gone so much. You saw me with the baby that day you stopped over to tell Daran about the phone call, and you assumed I was Larry's wife and that the baby was our child. Daran thought the same thing. Now you know the real situation. I'm not married and I don't have any chil—"

"Does Daran know that you're not Larry's wife?"

"Oh, yeah, he knows now," Star had said, recalling his verbal attack in the restaurant and how she'd shut his mouth.

Cordy, being acutely intuitive, had quickly grasped the implication that there'd been a scene of sorts. She chuckled, coming over to where Star stood beside the rattan chair. "Then that's another thing you and I have in common," Cordy said. "Neither of us is married yet. You, Larry, and your sister can help me with my plan and maybe I can help you find a husband." She patted Star's shoulder consolingly as she looked out over the dips and peaks of the vast Delaware farmland, muttering almost to herself, "We'll have to figure out a way to get married before, as my daddy says, we're 'left on the shelf.' "

Cordy watched Star's slim frame pass around the long curve that led to the throat of the spoon. There, where the land rose to its highest point, she noticed that Star slowed down considerably.

Now Cordy's mind raced. So Star wasn't married to Daran's friend. Instinctively she knew that this simple fact could cause a glitch in her plans. She suspected Daran found Star attractive. Star was certainly his type. And she was an American just like his ex-wife. What was there about those women that attracted him?

Something nagged at the edge of Cordy's mind. Her brow furrowed as her brain sifted through the past few days, searching for what had fueled her suspicions.

Then Cordy recalled the two of them sitting on the veranda that day when she'd gone over to tell him about the phone call. He'd been expecting that call! Yet there he sat, chatting with his friend's wife, or so she'd thought then. At that time she hadn't attached much significance to the incident. It hadn't seemed extraordinary. Before he left that day, he told her that he was going to drop off some lights at his friend's place, but that he'd be back in a few minutes because of the call from the Ivory Coast he was expecting at one-thirty. The call had come at two. Cordy had glanced out the window and spotted his car still parked on the hill at Larry's house. She asked the international operator to tell the caller to call back in fifteen minutes. Then she'd gone to get him.

And he'd gone over there again last night, Cordy thought. She'd heard him start his car and had watched as he drove over to Larry's house. Once again, there wasn't anything unusual about his visiting a friend. She remembered how she'd wished he'd at least asked her if she wanted to go along, just to meet Larry and his wife.

"Hm," Cordy intoned as she watched Star get the newspaper from the box and then cut across the lawn and go into the house. I wonder what she's thinking. Is she thinking about Daran? Is he thinking about her?

Cordy remembered how cheerful but restless he'd been when he came from his neighbors' house the night before. She wondered what had caused this mood, but when she tried to talk to him, he'd been short with her. At the time she thought he was still upset about what she'd done a few nights before. When she had gone ahead and tried to put her plan into operation. She felt she had no choice. She couldn't put it off any longer.

So she went into his room and then crept into his bed, pressing her nude body next to his as he slept. She had been delighted when he'd become instantly aroused. He fondled her feverishly and had almost mounted her before he'd realized what he was doing and to whom. He had tried to roll off her, but she held him tightly, parting her legs and moving her bottom in such an inviting way that his instincts had taken over and allowed him to enjoy her soft flesh momentarily.

Then he jumped from the bed and bellowed so loudly she thought the neighbors, though acres away, might have heard. He continued his tirade as he'd fumbled to turn on the bedside lamp, switching to their mother tongue.

"What are you doing? What are you doing here?" His voice had lowered a few decibels, but his flaring nostrils and his grimace of outrage had more than let Cordy know he was beside himself with anger.

She'd taken refuge under the sheet, watching him march around the room, gesturing wildly. The light from the lamp had given him a melodramatic appearance.

"What would Cheghum think of me? His best friend. If he could see us now…his sister…" He stabbed the air with his finger, pointing at her as he railed. "His own sister, as naked as the day she was born, in my bed? What would your family think? What would my family, friends, and business associates think? Have you forgotten that you're an African woman, Cordelia? We are Africans, and though we have lived in this country for a very long time, we are still Africans. I'm an African man. I'm not a weak-willed or wayward man who'll use your body to please myself and say to heck with the consequences. You know that in our culture, I would be held responsible for seducing a young woman who has been entrusted into my care by her family. Even if we did marry, your family would feel betrayed. I, not you, would be held responsible. Nobody would even listen if I told them you threw yourself at me. We both know our people would destroy me and dishonor my whole family's reputation far and wide. Everybody in the country who can talk would be talking about me. My business would be shattered. My dignity would be taken, and for what? A few minutes between your legs. No, no, never. There are too many other women who are made the same way you are. And if you ever—"

"And if I ever what, Daran? See, that's the problem. You think I'm some little child who doesn't know up from down. You're still looking at me like I'm a little girl. I'm thirty-one damn years old, Daran!" Cordy shrieked. She stood up then, still clutching the sheet close around her body.

"Maybe in the eyes of you men, women are always girls. We have the babies, we raise them, we run the household, we help support the family, we make sure that our children have all their needs met, forsake our own needs, and die in childbirth at an alarming rate around the world to have the babies that you selfish men want us to have to meet your needs. Yet you men have such fragile egos you can't give us credit for being more than your equal because that would make you feel too small and unnecessary. In the eyes of you men, we are these troublesome, greedy, complaining women who act like girls all our lives."

Cordelia could not remember ever having been so furious. It wasn't just that Daran had spurned her advances. It was so much more. The words that had spilled from her mouth surprised her, but damn it, she meant them. It had felt good to get all that frustration out.

She let the sheet drop, baring her heaving breasts and ripe curves.

Daran had flinched initially, but then he had looked her up and down. "Am I suppose to salivate?" he asked, smiling, calm even. "Cordelia, cover yourself. I know that you have all the right equipment."

"Yes, Daran. All the right equipment, but nobody wants it. Who will marry me? All the men my age at home will feel I'm too educated for them, and all the educated men will feel I'm too old. Thirty-one and on the shelf."

Picking up the sheet, she slowly draped it around her form. "You know my daddy will be coming soon and he'll be sure to tell me about a bunch of old men who want to marry me for their third, fourth, or fifth wife."

"Cordy, it doesn't have to be that way," Daran had said quietly. "Don't feel sorry for me, Daran. I would make you a good wife—not like Elaine."

"Cordelia, that's not your business," he cautioned.

But she continued anyway. "I'm strong, Daran. We have the same background, the same values, the same everything. Not like Elaine. You'll have to get married again. Why not me?"

"Whether I will marry again is not something I will talk to you about, Cordelia, and I don't plan to talk with you about anything else at this hour." He looked at the luminous dial of the digital bedside clock. "It's two-thirty in the morning. You know I have an early morning flight to New York. So leave. I need to sleep." He moved toward the doorway of the bedroom as if to show her the way.

Cordy moved toward the door but stopped just as she reached him. Then she moved so close to him that she felt his body heat. Her eyes had searched his face for any sign he might be weakening.

"Cordelia, your behavior is shameful and you're wasting my time. Go to bed." She heard the fatigue in his voice and had known that whatever might happen between them in the future wouldn't happen that night.

"That's okay," she said, strolling toward the door. "One time or the other, you'll do what you wanted to do tonight before your conscience and fear took over. Let's face it. You're a healthy, normal man with needs. You need a woman, and you know it just as well as I do. So I'll be back."

"That's up to you." His voice crackled with anger again. "But remember this: if I want to commit suicide, I wouldn't choose to do it by rolling in bed with you. Because we both know without a doubt that a roll in bed with you would be an exercise in my self-destruction."

A hot retort had crossed her mind, but he had switched off the bedside light and she could see by the dim hallway light that he'd gotten into bed, with his back to her. She swallowed her words.

She'd known it wouldn't be easy. He was a strong-willed man. But she, too, was strong, and desperate. And she was willing to do whatever she had to in order to avoid the supreme and permanent embarrassment of being one of an old man's many wives.

—⁄⁄⁄—

The morning's events weighed heavily on Starmaine as she entered the foyer. The house was as quiet as she had left it-not surprising, since Gail's philosophy was that a Sunday in bed was a day well spent. Apparently this credo had been absorbed by little Nanette too.

The morning had indeed been eventful, but if someone had asked Starmaine if her morning had gone well, she could not have given a clear-cut yes or no answer. She had certainly gotten the answers she sought. Well, at least she knew that Cordy lived with Daran and most likely they were lovers.

Cordy's plan was shocking enough, but the clincher was that she wanted Star, Gail, and Larry to help her with it. The woman certainly didn't lack for nerve.

The distasteful image of Daran making love to Cordy rose up in Star's mind. Cordy had all but said that they were lovers. Star thought of Daran's hard, muscular body, his smooth dark chocolate skin, and the intimate looks and soft whispers he directed at her when others weren't around. She squirmed and wondered if he looked at Cordy the same way, spoke to her the same way. Probably did. After all, intimate looks and soft whispers were probably just all part of a well-honed technique designed to guarantee a woman's capitulation. Not that he needed any of that with Cordy. Well, he's very definitely wasting his time with me, Star decided, no matter how intensely female he makes me feel.

After Lance, she promised herself she'd never again be used and abused by a fickle man. Before she could stop it, Aunt Mellie's old saying about women who slept with men before marriage flitted through her mind: "Why buy the cow when you can get the milk for free?"

Star hated to think of her relationship with Lance like that, but some men still thought that way. With Lance, what she'd thought was a deep, committed relationship on both their parts was something he'd dismissed with ease. He'd promised marriage. Well, he got married all right, but to someone else. And left her to learn his plans from the grapevine. Maybe his wife had held out for marriage. Star now realized how young and dewy-eyed she'd been where Lance was concerned. She had not really known anything about deep commitments then.

This whole thing called "deep commitment" had to be scrutinized all the time anyway. It seemed you always had to be on guard to see if lust was being mistaken for love. She'd given herself freely to Lance after he'd sworn they were meant to be together. Well, she'd been hurt badly and deeply embarrassed by tile whole episode, especially when people gave her pitying looks. But she was wiser and tougher as a result. That would never happen to her again. If a mutual attraction existed between her and a man, she'd accept it for what it was: lust, not love.

All of which brought her right back to her current dilemma with Daran Ajero. No man she'd ever met had the kind of raw appeal that Daran possessed. For the first time, she thoroughly understood how people were swept away by sheer lust.

Whenever that man was around, she became overheated and couldn't act natural. And he knew it, too. He made that clear. Men like him always seemed to have an uncanny way of knowing exactly what their effect on women was. If she weren't extremely careful she could end up being his woman over here while he had a woman over there. That wasn't about to happen but if it did, she would see it for what it was—not love, not commitment, just lust.

And besides, since Cordy had decided that the man just had to marry her, Star considered him off limits. And just as well, she concluded. He had an overwhelming appeal that could be dangerous to someone resolved to avoid emotional entanglements. Someone like her. Even if it killed her, she would force herself to be only neighborly and friendly toward him. Once she moved out of Gail and Larry's house, she would see him only occasionally when she came to visit, if then. The comforting thing was that once he was out of sight, she would put him clear out of her mind.

As Star lay back on the cushioned chaise lounge and gazed at the front page of the newspaper, exhaustion overcame her and she dozed off. A soft breeze blew through a small open panel alongside one of the floor-to-ceiling Palladiun windows Gail had chosen to grace both ends of the spacious family room. The breeze caused a billowing of the window's jabot curtains; the newspaper dropped on Star's still form, and the house was silent and peaceful except for the faint snores of its occupants.

CHAPTER 5

Some time later, the telephone next to the chaise rang, jarring Star awake. She grabbed it quickly, as she usually did. Gail never answered the phone and kept the answering machine set to pick up on the second ring. So Star was accustomed to acting fast.

Even half asleep, Star instantly recognized the man's voice on the line as that of Daran Ajero. His deep voice made the instrument come alive in her hand.

Somehow, she wasn't surprised it was he. Had she expected him to call? "Hello, Starmaine," he said. "I'm happy you answered the phone."

Star could hear the smile in his voice and she remembered the way his eyes danced when he smiled.

"Who's calling?" Star said. She could've kicked herself for pretending not to recognize his voice, but she needed some time to collect her wits. The man's voice—the man himself—had such a worrisome effect on her.

He chuckled. "As if you didn't know. But let's playa game. I'll give you some clues, and you get to guess who I am. Won't that be fun?"

"I don't play games." "I was at your house last night. We kissed and you wanted me to touch you all over. Guess who?"

Starmaine clutched the receiver in one hand while the nails of the other dug into her palm. Seconds passed while she tried to contain her growing annoyance and excitement.

"Another clue: I can't remember anything I said last night to your sister after you left the room. It was all I could do not to follow you. We…" He cleared his throat. "Starmaine, we need to spend some time together…alone. Starmaine, Starmaine." His voice trailed into a whisper.

She felt as if he was touching her. She began to talk to push him away and bring some reality back to the situation. "Daran, there are complications. I can't get involved with anyone now."

"Don't tell me lies, lady. Your sister told me you don't have a man in your life now."

She was furious at Gail for discussing her with him and furious at him and at people in general for thinking that a woman always needed a man in her life to be happy.

Now wide awake, she shot back, saying, "Please, suh, don't feel pity for this po' desperate female. She don't want no man in her life 'cause she don't need one."

He chuckled. "Okay, you've made your point. Now I know where you stand. But now that you've made yourself clear, there's nothing to keep us from going out sometimes. I won't touch you as long as you don't touch me or want me to touch you. You have my word on that and that's something I don't give without thought—in business or any other part of my life."

Thinking of Cordy, Star wanted to challenge this, but he'd called her bluff. Besides, what better way to prove to him and herself that she could resist this man than to go out with him?

"Sure. Why not," she said nonchalantly. "I'll pick you up tonight at eight. We'll do something casual. Good-bye, Starmaine."

Starmaine sat there for a long moment holding the humming receiver in her hand. She wasn't at all sure if she had handled the situation or if she herself had been handled.

Star was annoyed with herself for being nervous about their outing that evening. It was not a date. She refused to call it that. Still, as the hour approached, she couldn't decide what to wear. He said casual. What did that mean? Was it casual, meaning jeans or a simple dress?

She replayed their conversation over in her mind many times, examining his subtleties, his innuendos. She had to admit that she was titillated by him. He excited her and this worried her.

By six o'clock, she wanted to call him and claim she had a headache. She did, after all, get heat headaches, and the weather had been unseasonably warm. But what if he wasn't home? What if Cordy answered the phone? Gail had gotten up not long after he'd called. She'd told Star about Daran's interest in her. Star had behaved as nonchalantly as she could, saying he'd probably been just making conversation, though she admitted she'd agreed to take a drive with him that evening, just to be neighborly.

"Hm. I wonder why he didn't ask me to come along? I'm his neighbor, too," Gail said, her eyes wide with mock wonder.

When Star had begun to protest, Gail had put up a hand to stop her, saying, "Star, just enjoy yourself, girl. You work so hard, you don't have the social life you deserve. And here I've got you holed up out here in the country helping me, when you should be back in Philly living the life of a young single woman."

"Gail, don't start that again. We're family. That says it all. And now you've gone and got this guy thinking that I'm some kind of down-and-out female. Besides, he's already involved with someone." She watched Gail's mouth fall open. "I'll tell you all about that later. But the important thing is, that makes him a safe man to be friends with."

Gail had laughed, saying, "My beauty sleep this morning must've really paid off if I look young enough to swallow that. You go on and get ready for your date with your safe man. The only other thing I want to say about this whole matter is be careful."

Star finally managed to decide what to wear, choosing a navy-blue print jumpsuit made from a soft fabric—cool, yet elegantly casual. Her burnished copper loafers and a matching pendant and bracelet set it off spectacularly, she thought.

She had just stuck a bejeweled, copper-colored comb into one side of her hair when she heard the doorbell ring.

"I'll get it," she yelled through the intercom to Gail, who was down in the basement rec room playing with little Nanette. She grabbed her small shoulder bag and walked from her bedroom to the top of the staircase.

Suddenly her stomach began to flutter and her heart raced dangerously: She paused a moment to calm herself. "Starmaine," she lectured herself aloud, "you are a country girl, and a country girl does what she has to do. Right now you have to go on down to that door, open it, and face that man. You have to treat him so casually that he'll know that he's no big thing to you. You know you can do it. You've had to face whole rooms of arrogant people. You handled them and you can handle him."

Steeling herself, she sailed gracefully down the stairs. She could see him peering at her through the sidelight windows as she approached the door. A bevy of new flutters threatened to make her stomach lurch, but she pushed them down with every ounce of her will, and opened the door with a pleasant expression on her face.

She was relieved when she saw that he was dressed in a foam green polo shirt and khaki slacks. At least she'd dressed appropriately.

"Hello, Starmaine," he said in that soft voice of his.

She trembled slightly, unnoticeably, she hoped.

She looked up into his sparkling wine-brown eyes and said, "Hi, Daran, how are you?" Stepping out onto the· porch, she turned from him to make sure the door was shut, but then remembered that she hadn't told Gail she was leaving. "Back in a sec," she said and reentered the foyer, but that was as far as she got. Gail stood at the end of the foyer, grinning broadly at her.

Mildly annoyed, Star said, "What's with the look?" Not waiting for the answer, which she knew all too well, she said, "Just wanted to let you know I'm leaving. I shouldn't be out late."

Gail waved, mouthing a silent good-bye.

Daran had taken a seat in one of the porch chairs, but he stood up as she stepped back out on the porch.

"You're beautiful," he intoned softly as he gazed at her. "Thank you, Daran. Now, where are we off to? I told Gail I wouldn't be out late."

"Well you can't be sure of that," he said and took her arm, guiding her to his car. She noted he still had not told her where they were going. Did it really matter?

She hadn't felt this carefree for quite a while now. Always knowing could become very routine and boring. The mystery of their destination just lent that much more excitement to the night.

Like the gentleman she suspected him to be, he opened the car door for her and waited until she was in and settled before he shut the door and told her to lock it. Then he got in and they were off.

As the car turned onto the wide handle portion of the spoon-shaped road, Star couldn't help but glance back at his house. Cordy weighed heavily on her mind. She had to admit she felt guilty about this innocent outing with the man that Cordy was determined to marry.

Well, she believed in getting things out into the open. "Guess who I had a long talk with today?" she asked as they reached the main highway.

"Well let's see. Hm, it must have been Cordelia," he replied, turning to smile at her before driving smoothly out onto the interstate highway.

Feeling like a comedian whose punch line had been stolen, she plowed on. "Yes. She told me about all the things you two have in common and the things you share."

They were on Route 13 now. It was completely dark except for the headlights of the other cars, but she saw him glancing at her.

"Oh, I know Cordelia can really talk a lot," he said. "But it's common knowledge that we share a country of origin, and having both grown up there, we share the same culture."

"Well, she did tell me that, but she talked mainly about the things the two of you share in this country."

"Oh, naturally we share a house at the present time. Hopefully, that situation will change soon." Star was angry. She thought he was being deliberately evasive. "Oh, she told me a lot more than that-personal things," Star added, hoping to flush him out. It worked.

"Yes, I'm sure she told you about our marriage plans and our fabulous life together afterwards."

Star was silent.

"Well, did she?"

"She did, and frankly, it was disturbing."

"Why were you disturbed? Were you jealous?"

Thanks to the car's darkened interior, Star didn't have to worry too much about hiding her facial expression—only her tone of voice. "Now, really, Daran, only a man who's in love with his own charm would think I'd be jealous. Or should I say charms?"

He chuckled. "No, Starmaine, I'm just very good at reading people. I'm very honest about my feelings about you, but you—"

"Oh, golly gee, I'm sure I should be thankful that you have feelings for me. And what feelings are those,

Daran Ajero? Are those the feelings that make a man hotly pursue a woman until he gets her body? Or do your feelings keep you pursuing until you also have her mind and soul, too? And then I suppose you're off to the next conquest."

"Starmaine, I'm not that kind of man." He paused and cleared his throat. "I've been hurt myself."

Starmaine wasn't ready to hear about his pain. Her own disastrous experience with Lance was threatening to rise up.

"Okay, Daran. Let's just enjoy ourselves on this mystery trip you're taking me on. Can't you give me a clue?" she asked as the car sped south on Route 13.

"Now, why would I want to do that?" he teased. "Just sit back and enjoy the ride."

She had to admit she really was enjoying herself. He was such a self-assured, charming man. Somehow, she felt he could handle any situation anywhere. He had certainly managed to handle this situation, because here she sat in his car while he had a woman who planned to marry him living in his house.

She had to remember that, despite the way he'd tried to paint it. This is just an innocent outing. He can't do anything to me if I don't let him, she pointed out to herself.

Moments later he took hold of her hand, but she jerked hers away. When she stole a look his way, his eyes remained fixed on the road.

He chuckled and said softly, "Starmaine, are you afraid of me? Why are you pulling away?"

"We are not on a date, remember? Holding hands was not part of the arrangement."

He sighed. "Starmaine, Starmaine. Why do you continue to act like this?" His voice was soft and caressing. "You know what I want to do? I want to stop at a motel right now and make love with you. I'm not hiding how I feel about you. I've had a full-blown fantasy about you ever since I set eyes on you. Let me share it with you."

"Daran, just keep your mind on the driving," she lectured like a schoolmarm. She could feel a knot beginning to tighten in the pit of her stomach. No, it had been there ever since she had seen him outside the door this evening. She had thought talking about Cordy would force it away, but that certainly hadn't worked. The knot was just getting tighter. She clenched her fists and pressed them into the leather seat to control this feeling as he kept talking.

"Starmaine." His tone was that of an exasperated adult patiently contending with a small child. "You won't let me touch you even though you want me to. At least let me tell you how desirable you are to me."

Intense emotions swirled through the car. Star was rapidly approaching the end of her tether. "How do you know?" she said. "I mean, just how do you know I want you to touch me? You're full of conceit, Daran. That's a big problem of yours. Just drive!"

He ignored her remarks and continued in a tone that had become both annoying and mesmerizing. "I'm out in the forest one day and I happen upon you, except that you're a wood nymph. Like all wood nymphs, you are completely naked." He paused and swallowed before continuing. "You're completely free of inhibitions, pretenses, and guile."

Star laughed, more to hide her growing excitement than because she found anything humorous about his fantasy. She said, "I sure hope you act like a complete gentleman."

"Oh, I'm always a gentle man, Starmaine. At any rate, I've been fishing, and there I sit, cooking the fish, when I notice someone lurking around my campsite. I investigate and find you, stunningly female and splendidly naked, hiding behind a tree."

"Well, at least I have enough sense to hide."

"I invite you to come and share my food with me. You accept and you walk ahead of me to my camp. By this time, I'm fully aroused, but fortunately I'm wearing clothes and can hide my excitement."

And fortunately too, he can't see my face in this dark car, Starmaine thought, feeling warm and flushed though cool air blew directly on her through the car's air vents.

"We have lunch, and all the while we're chatting—"

"I wonder what we'd have to chat about, since I'm so innocent and naive."

"Well, in a fantasy things don't have to make sense. Anyway, after we've eaten, you get very curious about my tent and you begin to poke at it. You go inside, and seeing my bed, you lie down on it. I can see you lying on it from outside the tent where I'm still sitting, restraining myself from following you. I see you draw your legs up and I can't control myself any longer. I go into the tent and kneel down next to you. You look at me and start to laugh softly, enchantingly."

"I'm not sounding very naive if I'm lying naked on a man's bed, laughing softly at him as he kneels beside it."

"I begin to kiss your feet, your ankles, your legs and thighs. When I look at your face, you stare at me in wonder. I touch your center and you are moist. I begin to shed my clothes when suddenly I see another man in the corner. This man is naked and comes to the bed and is suddenly on you and in you and you begin to writhe. I wake up at this point, hard and furious."

"Sounds like you have some very vivid fantasies," Star said lightly to relieve the nearly suffocating heat and tension in the car. She leaned forward and fumbled, looking for the car stereo, but she wasn't able to find it.

Noticing what she was trying to do, he pressed one of the numerous buttons on the car's dashboard. A soft, romantic ballad filled the car.

"I'm in the mood for something faster than that," she said. No sooner had she spoken than the sound of a Miami band came through the powerful speakers.

She snapped her fingers to the beat and noticed that they had just crossed into the beach town of Windy Bay:

The town drew hordes of summer tourists who flocked to the beach, boardwalk, and trendy shops. During the winter, however, only its dozen or so seafood restaurants remained open, offering what was touted as the best seafood on the Eastern Seaboard. As it was already early October, most of the other businesses were already closed after the busy summer.

Star had heard much about what the town had to offer, but she'd never been there before. She took in the names and windows of the various shops along the long, winding main street. It looked like the kind of place she'd like to come back to and explore at leisure.

Minutes later, Daran slowed the car in front of a cedar and glass restaurant called the Tiger's Alley. From the numerous patrons she could see through the windows, Star could tell the restaurant was a popular eatery. She saw several black couples among those entering and among those busily eating.

"Look at all the black folks," Star said, turning toward Daran, who'd been silent for a while. "The food must be scrumptious."

"Yes, Tiger's staff is unbeatable. They specialize in Afro-Caribbean and West African dishes. People come from as far north as Philadelphia and as far south as Washington, D.C., just to eat at Tiger's. They get so loaded down with food they have to get a room for the night."

She glanced at him and he winked at her, adding, "Unfortunately, we don't come from that far."

Daran turned into a parking lot across the street and gave his key to one of the young attendants. Then he and Star walked the few steps to the intersection and waited for the light to change.

When the Walk light signaled them, Daran reached for her hand. Her first impulse was to pull away again, but she felt that would be silly. After all, she wasn't a shy young schoolgirl. What did it matter if he held her hand?

He grasped her hand with his long, firm fingers and held it securely, not letting go until he had to open the door of the restaurant. He ushered her in and they were met by a smiling middle-aged woman in African attire.

"Oh, Daran! How are you?" She said something in another language.

"Just working really hard and otherwise occupied," Daran answered in English while looking pointedly at Star. He turned to her, and said, "Starmaine, I'd like for you to meet Mrs. Abuji, Tiger's wife."

The two women shook hands and exchanged "pleased to meet you's." "Come with me," Mrs. Abuji said, leading the way past the bar area. "I know just where to put you so you won't be in a fishbowl."

They followed her to an elevated part of the restaurant that was softly lit and away from the heavily trafficked walkway. When they were seated, Starmaine noticed that they sat overlooking a river. The movement of the water made it seem as if they

were out on a boat. Starmaine even had a slight feeling
of seasickness. She shivered.

"Cold?" Daran asked, his hand covering her
clasped ones, resting on the table.

"No," she said, and smiled as she took a deep
breath. "I'm really enjoying myself. The atmosphere is
wonderful. This is like a faraway place, away from
both the congested streets of Philadelphia and the
Delaware farmlands. There's just nothing like being
near the water, whether it's a river or the ocean."

He regarded her enthusiasm with pleasure. "I'll
have to keep that in mind," he murmured, choosing a
celery stalk from the assortment of raw vegetables the
waitress had placed in the center of the table.

The waitress came back just moments later to
take their order. Star felt a little embarrassed. She
hadn't even glanced at the menu, but then neither had
Daran. Star looked at the waitress and grabbed the
menu, overwhelmed by the array of unfamiliar dishes
on it.

Thank goodness, there's an explanation beneath
the names, she thought. Daran let her scan the menu
before he asked, "May I order for you?"

She smiled and wagged her finger at him. "Yes,
you may, and you'd better order me something delicious because I am a hungry woman."

"No problem," he said. "You're out with an African, so you'll eat the way we do." He turned and said a few words to the waitress in that same beautiful language Star didn't understand. The waitress made notes on her pad and then was off.

"Is she an African?" Star asked.

"No, she's African American, but she's worked with Tiger and his wife for years now, from the time they had their first restaurant. Well, it wasn't even a restaurant; it was a food stand that sold African food. They used to haul it around in the back of their station wagon. After many years, it paid off and now—this," he said, gesturing at their handsome surroundings.

The food arrived. The meat and vegetable stew smelled delicious. Next came a mound of what looked like dough, and next to their plates, the waitress placed little aluminum bowls of water. There were no eating utensils on the table.

Daran noticed her confusion and explained that this dish was called efo egusi and the dough-like mound was called gari. He washed his fingers in the little aluminum bowl and showed her how to eat, using his fingers to scoop up a small amount of the dough and dipping it into the thick stew.

"Many Africans," he explained, "won't eat African dishes with their hands in public because they don't want Westerners to think they are primitive. They are brainwashed. Would someone Chinese eat his food in a Chinese restaurant with a knife and fork? No. Would a European go to the Russian Tea Room and eat with his hands? No. Then why won't an African go to an African restaurant and eat African food with his hands, the way his culture has taught him? Their minds have been tampered with," Daran said, touching his finger to his temple.

Star stole a look around her and saw that at several tables this was true. And surprisingly, she saw a white couple eating with their hands.

"But how do you know they are Africans? They might be from this country or from the Caribbean."

"Oh, I can always recognize a born and bred African," he explained. "I can see it in their body language, the subtle gestures and mannerisms."

"Truly amazing," she said, glancing around and wondering if she could identify the African Americans by watching the body movements of the restaurant's patrons.

"I want you to understand this about me, Starmaine. I'm an African and I'll always be an African, no matter how long I live in this country or anywhere else. One day, I'll go home to stay. The urge is always there. It's in them, too," he said, nodding his head at all the Africans in the restaurant.

"We enjoy the comfort and conveniences American technology provides, but we don't come here to stay: We come here to attend college, and after that's accomplished, we go home. For example, Tiger's cousin arrived here a few weeks ago to attend medical school at the University of Pennsylvania. He's already talking about building a small hospital at home when he returns. So you see, we're not immigrants. It's just that these days, there's so much corruption at home that we're staying here longer. If it wasn't for that, most of us would be home now."

Starmaine listened to him talk. She'd never seen this side of him. He'd always seemed so lighthearted before. Now she could see he was a man of strong convictions about his African identity and culture, his country, and possibly anything and anyone else with which he became involved.

She couldn't imagine him getting caught up in fads and trends. No, he was a firmly grounded man—grounded like a rock.

As he talked about the political situation in his country and the causes of the conflict on the African continent, she could sense that their relationship was changing. It was like he was drawing back the curtain to let her inside his private room. He was revealing himself to her. Or was he? Maybe he just wanted to talk about what was important to him and she happened to be the person there with him. But somehow, though she tried, she could not fully believe this. Though he acted like someone who didn't take things too seriously, she now suspected he wasn't casual at all, not when things and people really mattered to him.

It was all so heady. Star wasn't ready for this new aspect of him. He embodied so many questions. And there were still those cloudy pieces of his life, mostly centering around Cordy. She had to keep the Cordy situation in mind. She would never be a man's other woman. No matter how innocently he portrayed his relationship with Cordy, there was no escaping the fact that the young and very attractive woman lived with him. And Cordy had made it all too clear that she would stop at nothing to become his wife.

Since her experience with Lance, Starmaine had made it a policy to be brutally honest with herself. Honesty now demanded that she recognize all the signposts leading to disappointment and heartache. Daran was a man who had a strong sexual appetite; he'd made that clear. How could he live under the same roof with an inviting, desirable woman and not satisfy that appetite?

Undoubtedly he was receiving intense pressure from Cordy to marry her. Perhaps pursuing another woman was his way of avoiding making a commitment to Cordy while simultaneously having another outlet for his sexual appetite.

Who knew what was really happening in that house of his? It wouldn't be the first time a man had lied to get his way. And his being Larry's friend? Well, that wouldn't prevent Daran from sleeping with her. After all, if it happened, she would be a consenting adult. It wasn't Larry's business and she didn't want it to be. She didn't need Larry or anyone else to watch over her and protect her. Daran Ajero was a gigantic question mark. That was a fact. Being sensible about the situation dictated that she proceed with caution and leave all the exit doors open.

Well, so much for being sensible, she thought minutes later after she had agreed to take a ferry ride from the southern tip of Delaware over to Cape May, New Jersey. *What harm could it do?* she wondered. *What could possibly happen on a ferry?*

CHAPTER 6

Star reflected on the previous evening's occurrences the next morning as she drove to the support group meeting. This was the second meeting of the group and she wondered how it would go. They had decided to hold the meetings in each other's homes instead of at the community center because homes were more intimate.

Gwen was the member who'd offered her home for today's meeting, pointing out that some of the women did not receive much company at home, and this too was a need. The others had agreed, welcoming her gesture. Meeting with your "sisters" in their homes was certainly more natural and Star believed it would help make the group feel more like an extended family.

Star had been careful to stress at the initial meeting that she was not the group's leader. She'd said they were all responsible for the success of the group. Still, she knew the women would expect her to show them the next step. *What is the next step?* she wondered.

She made a right turn off Route 6 onto Skyterrace Heights Drive, following the directions Gwen had given. She still had two miles to go and since she was a little early, she decided to move into the slow lane and enjoy the scenery.

Some people claimed this section of New Castle County boasted the most beautiful land in the state. As the road curved, dipped and rose, so did the widely spaced houses. Some were perched high and others low, but they were all set back from the road and attractively framed by the trees, the land, and each other. The varying shades of red and yellow fall foliage were a striking complement to the landscape. It was as if an artist's brush had painted and strategically positioned them for a coordinated effect.

As Star approached the third traffic light, she moved into the left lane as instructed and then made the turn onto Gwen's street—Terrace Way. Star double-checked the address and parked her car at the curb. As she got out, she admired the gray fieldstone house and its small lawn. Two trees sported dark fuchsia leaves.

Gwen was one of the two married women in the group. But her husband worked in Washington. He was home only two days a week, sometimes on weekends and sometimes during the week. As Gwen had said, laughingly, "When Leroy is home, we are inseparable; he wants all of me and I want all of him."

Star assumed none of the cars she saw parked in the driveway and along the street in front of the house belonged to him. As she neared the front door, she heard familiar laughter streaming from the house. The sound reassured her.

She rang the doorbell, more for politeness than need—the varnished pine door had been left ajar. She called inside, "It's Star. I'm coming in."

"Come on in," the chorus of welcoming voices called back. Wiping her hands, Gwen emerged from a part of the house that apparently contained the kitchen. "Girl, how you doin'?" Gwen asked with a big smile, her arms stretched out in welcome. She gave Star a big hug and ushered her into the cozy living room. Star made the rounds, embracing each of the five women there. Only two of the women who had attended the initial meeting were not there.

As if reading her mind, Gwen said, "Angela called. She's running late but is on her way. And Cynthia called. She said she can't be in the group right now, but she didn't say why."

The women looked at each other. Then Doris, a stylishly dressed high school principal, said, "She must not need this group like we do."

"Or she just doesn't know what her needs are," added Printella, a sixtyish recent divorcée. Nodding, the women agreed that this was more likely the cause, and with that, the discussion was already underway.

Star felt exhilarated once again about starting the group. The level of honesty these women had about their basic need for one another impressed her and made her feel closer to them. They had all come together for the sole purpose of supporting each other and promoting each member's health and well-being. And hadn't research shown that people with more supportive, positive relationships were healthier? As she had hoped, the group was well on its way to developing as a substitute for the tightly knit extended family she'd known as a child. If this group was successful, couldn't other groups in different locales succeed as well?

As Star looked at the faces—some relaxed, some tense, others excited—she felt as if she was actually back in the small southern community where she'd grown up. This looked very much like the meetings the church sisters back home had, getting together to plan an upcoming revival or some other event.

Star took it all in as she and the others enjoyed the delicious food Gwen had prepared. Once they'd finished eating, they got down to what they had really come together for—sharing.

Gwen took the lead, saying, "Okay, Starmaine, what's happened to you since we last saw each other?"

Star hesitated, both startled and impressed by the ease with which Gwen had taken charge, and even more startled by being asked about herself. But she felt safe with these women and soon began talking. "There's this guy who's come into my life recently…" She paused and sighed, suddenly overwhelmed by a rush of frustrating emotions.

"And into your heart," Ida, the woman beside Star, prompted. "That's the problem," Star said softly as tumultuous emotions churned within her. "I'm afraid to let him into my heart. I'm scared to trust him completely and I'm the kind of woman who has to trust a man completely if I'm going to have a relationship with him." The image of Cordy rose in her mind.

"You see, there's a major complication," she continued. "There's another woman."

"Honey, tell us something we don't know," chimed in Alma, another of the group's older members. The other women chuckled, giving each other experience-laden looks.

"Does he tell you that he's just not a one-woman man?" Printella asked as she pursed her lips and rolled her eyes.

"Sh, sh, let Star talk," Gwen admonished gently. "Remember when a sister is talking, we have to let her get those emotions up. Give her space to feel them and wrestle with them so she can deal with them."

Bolstered by Gwen's support, Star continued, "First of all, he's an African. But he's not the one causing the problem, although he's a part of it. It's really the woman who's causing the problem because she's chasing him. She's an African woman and she's desperate to get married, so any man will do. You know the type. After all there're enough American women like that too." Some of the women chortled and nodded their heads.

"I just don't know. I just don't know," Star repeated as her frustration mounted. "Whenever I try to think this thing through I meet a brick wall."

Suddenly Ida took Star's hand in her own and squeezed it. "We're with you, Star. Go ahead and talk it out. We understand. This guy has got your motor running, but you don't know if you should take off with him."

"I don't know if he's sleeping with her," Star blurted. "But I do know that she's pursuing him, and frankly I've never heard of any man who can turn it down when a woman lives with him and can pitch it at him morning, noon, and night. She's got the motive and the opportunity and he's got the hormones. I don't plan to be any man's other woman."

"You mean this woman is *living* with this man and you're wondering whether you should get involved in a meaningful relationship with him? Starmaine, you are smarter than that," Alma stated flatly. "The next time he comes sniffing around you, tell that dog bye-bye." She waved her hand for emphasis.

The other women laughed and threw in their own versions of how they would tell a man like that to get lost.

"Sisters, I know you think you're helping me by giving me advice, but we want to support each other around our struggle to make the best decisions for ourselves. Each of us has to make her own decisions, no matter what any of the rest of us might think."

"Yeah," Doris chimed in. "That's why I'm here, to get support in dealing with craziness, because let's face it, sisters, we live in a crazy world. If you always do the straightforward, sensible thing in a crazy world, you don't get anywhere or you get grief. You have to know how to navigate around the land mines and dodge the sharks in order to get the gold."

"Speak, sister, speak!" the other women exhorted animatedly, and then they began to tell each other some of their more absurd experiences.

After giving them a few minutes to vent, Gwen said, "I have a hunch that we'll be hearing plenty about this man in Starmaine's life, so let's hear the who, how, where, what, and when about this guy. So, Star, tell it from the top."

Star took a deep breath and began to relay the details of the first and subsequent meetings between her and Daran. All of it flew from her mouth. Well, everything except his steamy fantasy. Some information was too personal even to tell your support group, she reasoned. But she did share the poignant moments she and Daran had spent together on the ferry.

Once Daran had parked his car on the ferry's bottom level, they'd climbed the stairs to the main deck. She recalled it all so vividly. The wonderful smell of the night ocean, the cool spray in her face. She and Daran strolled around the ferry from one end to the other. Many of the passengers did likewise, but after a while the others went inside or onto the upper deck. Daran steered her to an area of the boat's stern where they were alone. He took her hand and peered at her in the near darkness, but when she refused to return his gaze, he chuckled and squeezed her hand for a long moment.

She did not stop him. He could hold her hand if he wanted to. She reminded herself that she had to let this man know that he was no big deal. Jerking her hand from his would make him think the opposite.

"My mother was a very successful trader," he said, looking out over the dark Atlantic waters as if he could see his country. "When we were very young, she would rise early each morning and make breakfast for my dad and us. As soon as my daddy left for his job at the ship-yard, we would help her bundle up all her oranges, bananas, yams, and plantains. Then we'd go with her to one of the busy roads in Lagos where she'd join the other trading women. My two younger brothers and I would leave her there at the roadside and go to school. My little baby sister would spend the days wrapped on my mother's back while she went about her trading. After school, we would go back to meet her and help her carry home the things she hadn't sold.

"She did this every morning until she had saved enough to buy a stall at the huge market in Surulere in the center of Lagos. It's the biggest African market-place in West Africa, covering an area of at least fifteen acres."

He lowered his voice and spoke into her ear. "One day we'll stroll through that market together, Starmaine." He squeezed her hand tightly as they both watched the shoreline fade away behind the ferry.

As the boat drew further from the shore, inky blackness surrounded them save for the faint lights from the ferry's interior. Though she couldn't see his eyes, she could feel him gazing at her. "Africa is one of those places I'd like to visit," Star said noncommittally.

He chuckled again. "Starmaine, you're still pushing me away. It would be so much more fun if you'd just let your guard down and relax with me."

She was silent, unwilling to engage in a contest of words or wills, and his voice continued in the misty darkness.

"My mother became very successful at trading. Even today, she can negotiate a better deal than a lot of corporate sharks. It was the money she made that paid my tuition at the American school there and my college tuition over here."

"Didn't your father feel jealous about your mother's success?"

"No, our culture is different. There a person's status is not determined by how much money he or she makes but by fulfilling a preordained role in the culture. As long as the person performs that role, no status is lost. There is no need to compete with someone with a different role. You are too busy trying to perform your own. So it never occurred to my father to compete with my mother, and he never felt any less of a man because of her success at trading."

"Isn't that because being a man in Africa is a privilege in itself, whereas a woman can win a Nobel Prize and she's still just a woman?"

"Spoken like a true Westerner."

"Well, that's what I am!" she retorted.

"It's like this, Starmaine. In our culture…"

Our meant his and Cordy's, Star thought, only half listening to him. Their culture—it's something Cordy shares with him that I could never fully share. I have to remember that. And remembering Cordy's desperate goal to marry the man made Star ask herself why she had really gone out with him. Showing him he was no big thing suddenly seemed ridiculous. The essence of the man brushed such child's play away as if it were a feather.

Daran kept talking, saying now, "The oldest son has a role in the family that no other child can assume. Even if the younger child can perform the role better, it is still the oldest child's responsibility to do that role."

"Sounds kind of rigid."

"Maybe from a Westerner's viewpoint, but actually, there's a lot of elasticity built in as well. It's a very old culture and very comprehensive. Although we were colonized by the West, the family and the bond between its members was never violated. So the most important aspect of our culture—or of any culture— escaped the colonizers' grasp. And you must remember, Starmaine, family encompasses a much larger circle of people in Africa. We don't have words in our language for first, second, and third cousins. To my mother, all of those cousins are her sister's children, whether there's a sister in Western terms or not. She embraces them all equally. When Africans go abroad, our friends become our family and we treat them accordingly. Any African can come to my door and I must feed the person and give him a place to stay or find him a place to stay if I'm able to do so. That's the culture. The culture is me."

"That's really wonderful," Star murmured.

"Our indigenous political and economic relationships and legal system were destroyed, however. That's why you see the current disarray in Africa. It's like we're trying to wear the clothes of foreigners and they don't fit us. But we will rebuild because the most important part of us was left untouched: those roles, the respect for our elders, and that family bond between Africans. Starmaine, that's our strength, the pillar of our culture and our future."

It certainly is a different type of place, Starmaine thought as she compared their two cultures. Aunt Mellie had been the matriarch of their family. The old woman's wisdom and strength had been the guiding hands, ensuring that the various brothers and sisters and their children adhered to the "down home" commonsense values and customs. Aunt Mellie had been the glue that made the family stick together to celebrate or weather the storms of the family's highs and lows.

Now with Aunt Mellie gone, many in the family had become wayward, pulled by fads and strains, and the notion of "doing your own thing." And when you looked at the situation, as Star had been doing more and more lately, no one was any better off for it. She craved the feeling of belonging to a community and connecting with a large group of like-minded people who shared her values. As a small girl and teenager growing up in the Deep South, she had taken all of that for granted. She'd even thought it to be old-fashioned and stifling. Now she felt entirely different. How comforting it must be for Daran and Cordy to know that there were tens of millions of fellow Africans who believed, as Aunt Mellie had, that the family was all-important.

"Anyway, after college I went home and worked for an oil company for a while," Daran continued. "Then I set up my own engineering and business consultancy. It was just the right time for my type of business there. I was successful in getting some big contracts quickly. I made a lot of money. I still make a lot of money performing necessary services."

"What exactly do you do?"

"Actually I do the same kind of work my mother did. Buy and sell. Only I deal in different, more expensive, and sometimes less tangible items—everything from Boeing airplanes to mainframe computers. Sometimes I buy and sell currency or favors. I'm a broker, a facilitator. There's a tremendous amount of trading that goes on between Africa and the West. I've been involved in a lot of big deals and I get a percentage." He broke off. "Enough about me. Tell me about your work. It's different."

His voice in the darkness and his closeness coupled with the rocking of the boat and her own turbulent feelings gave the scene an unreal, dreamy quality. She had the frightening feeling that something was about to happen and she could not prevent it from happening. She kept trying to outrun it, but it stayed close on her heels. She was tired of all this running. She was tired of running from him.

But what if she stopped? That would be worse. At times like tonight—when she yearned to be held, to be enveloped in a man's arms and have her body envelop his, to stop struggling with her heart and admit her feelings—she couldn't help thinking that those few moments of bliss would exact a heavy toll. No, she wouldn't stop struggling. Struggling eternally to keep him at bay was preferable to letting him get too close and trusting him as she had Lance.

As she talked about her job's more glamorous aspects as well as its more tedious ones, she couldn't help but appreciate the attentive way he listened and asked thoughtful questions. At first she thought he was just being polite, but when several of her answers sparked forays into other avenues, she realized that he was genuinely interested in what she did and how she felt.

"Do you have men in any of these classes that you conduct?" he asked.

"Sure. Some of the classes are coed. But I don't actually conduct classes anymore. I design aerobic and general fitness programs for clubs, spas, and resorts; then I have to implement and manage every aspect of the program I've designed. That involves hiring aerobics teachers, teaching them, and troubleshooting the whole operation so that everything runs smoothly. Currently I manage the four Placido locations in Wilmington and the Philadelphia area. And if I get a tempting enough offer, I sometimes consult for other companies. Believe me, it's a lot more involved than what I once did."

"Well, I can imagine why some of those guys keep going," he remarked, implying that the men were there to meet women. "Did you ever meet anyone—a guy, I mean—that you liked in any of those classes?"

"When I'm working, I'm all professional and a very hard driver." She chuckled.

"I've been told my whole personality changes. Besides, the men are there to get their workout, and a bunch of sweaty men and women are not very appealing. Take my word for it, meeting women is not the reason they keep coming."

"Men are always interested in meeting women, Starmaine. Like the day I first came by the house. I did not go there to meet you, but after I met you, I certainly wanted to see you again despite the guilt that I felt about being attracted to my friend's wife. And now here we are. It would have been the same thing at the club."

Star's mind went back to their first meetings, at the supermarket and then at the house. She swayed at the memory of the electricity that had ripped through her when his lips touched her skin. She admitted to herself that he was a very exciting man, a man she would welcome into her life under the right circumstances. But the very fact that he was coming on to her while Cordy sat waiting in his house was proof that he spelled trouble. And there were all those cultural differences. A relationship was hard enough when the man and woman came from the same background.

I must be out of my mind for even thinking about a relationship, she concluded. And before she realized it, a mournful sigh escaped her.

"What's wrong? Are you cold?" He was instantly solicitous. Warm fingers gripped her arm in the dark and guided her to him. He stood leaning back against the ferry's waist-high railing. His arms encircled her waist and he pulled her against him. Star was jolted by the delicious wave of heat blasting from his body into hers. Her lips parted as she drank in the moment—the masculine smell and feel of him. She shivered and his body shifted in order to pull her closer. He cupped the back of her neck in his hand. His lips trailed feathery kisses from her forehead down her cheek to her still-parted lips. With the tip of his tongue, he played at the corners of her mouth before plunging his tongue inside, probing the slippery softness he found there. He groaned as his excitement intensified, and she felt the hard evidence of his heightened emotion press against her.

But when his other hand began to stroke beside the soft curve of her breast, Star pulled back from him.

"Okay, Starmaine," he whispered, instantly removing his hand. "I won't touch you there, but just let me hold you." His deep voice vibrated with emotion, tempting Star. But then the little voice inside reminded her of the mistake she'd made before.

"No, Daran. A kiss is just a kiss, and we'll leave it at that," she said, pulling away from him. "It doesn't mean anything and it doesn't solve anything."

"What's there to solve? I'm not married and you're not either. What's wrong with our kissing and touching each other?"

"You may not be married, but you're not available and you know it! No matter how innocent you claim your relationship with Cordy is, I refuse to be sucked into a triangle."

"Starmaine, why won't you just believe me? Whatever you think is going on between Cordelia and me is in her imagination and now yours. Cordelia is— how shall I say it? She's odd sometimes. She has various boyfriends, but for her own peculiar reasons, she finds something wrong with them all. She's rude to them when they call. Whenever they're around, she treats them bad, and finally they give up. It's become a habit with her, and just like any habit, it's become more fixed over time. On top of that, she's developed that fixation of hers that she and I will marry one day."

"Daran, I don't want to talk about it. Let's go back inside," she said, turning to leave.

He followed her in tense silence as they moved toward the front of the ferry. From the lights that were still far off in the distance, Star knew they were about halfway between the Delaware and the New Jersey coasts.

As they sat on one of the comfortable deck benches that lined the bulwark, he broke the tension. "Tell me more about your job. How did you get started?"

Star grasped at this attempt to get the conversation back in balance and launched into an account of how her lifelong interest in health had led her into the fitness field and to her current job at the Placido.

When she finished, he shook his head. "In Africa, people would say that you're a loose woman—a prostitute. No man in his right man would let his wife work in a place like that."

Star bristled and swiveled her head toward him. His silhouette was outlined by the light from the boat's restaurant. "Well, since I'm a grown woman, I decide where I'm going to work—married or not."

He chortled. "Do I detect a feminist lurking beneath that very feminine exterior?"

"You can call me anything you want, but I believe a grown woman should decide what and where she does what she does or doesn't do. No man has the right to dictate anything to a woman. Women are not children. And any man that tried to treat me like a child would not have me around for long." Star was fuming. He'd touched one of her pet peeves.

"That's why there're so many divorces in this coun—"

"No, Daran. The reason there are so many divorces is because people don't communicate how they really feel about the most important issues. And because men don't want to give up their position as lord and master and treat women like full-fledged human beings!"

"Starmaine, everybody has a role to play."

"But that's just it. You're in America now. Women play every role. Women can and actually do everything men do, but they're still treated like afterthoughts."

"Starmaine, I am an enlightened man. I know that a lot of things are unfair sometimes, even in Africa, but it sounds like you're saying that women are superior to men."

You're quick, she thought, but she pressed her lips together just in time to prevent the sarcastic words from jumping out. Instead, she said, "What I'm saying is that credit ought to be given where credit is due. If I can do more things or get something done better than you, then it's fair for me to get the chance, the recognition, the praise, and the compensation. But these days a lot of women have a full-time job outside the home, and when they come home they have another full-time job—the second shift, the house-work and the kids. After all of that, they have another shift: they have to take care of their husband's needs."

"Starmaine, you're forgetting that a lot of women love cooking and doing things around the house."

"Don't bet on it!" she rebutted. "I, for one, hate cooking and housecleaning with a passion. That's not what I was put on this earth for. A lot of women feel the same way I do, but they wouldn't dare tell a man that for fear he would think she's one of those terrible women's libbers. So she marries him, hoping that he'll be fair and that things will work out. But, just like you, he's thinking she will be thrilled to be a cook and housekeeper."

"Would you also hate having babies?" he asked softly.

Starmaine felt suddenly warm. "Babies? I'm not talking about babies."

"But I am. How do you feel about having children?"

"We're talking about something totally different." Star was uncomfortable and wanted to get off the topic.

"No, we're not. Sometimes men and women get married and have babies. That has been known to happen. It even happened with Gail and Larry."

"Leave it to a man to try to change the subject, especially when discussing how unfairly men treat women."

"Starmaine, you said a few minutes ago that a lack of truthful communication is one reason for the high divorce rate in the country. I think you've got something there and I want to pursue it."

"I wasn't talking about us. We are not married, Daran!" *You're already spoken for, even if I were interested,* Star wanted to add.

"But, communication is important even among friends like us, isn't it, Starmaine?"

Damn, the man wouldn't let up! "I love babies. All right! I plan to have at least two! Do you want to know what their names will be?"

"No. That's not necessary That'll be decided at the right time. You've answered my question. There's nothing like good, old-fashioned honesty between friends."

Star would not be placated. "For their own selfish reasons, honesty is something a lot of men have a problem with when it comes to women. And, I admit, women are the same sometimes, but for different reasons. I'm not a game player. Games aren't for me because there can only be one winner, and what happens if I'm not it?" Lance won and I was devastated, she answered silently. "So I'm only too happy to let a man know where I stand."

"Well, no man can ever say that you didn't warn him. I like that. And I like your ideas about things. They're challenging. I prefer a woman who says what's on her mind, and you certainly don't have a problem with that—at least sometimes."

Starmaine refused to question the meaning of this last remark. That would take them into dangerous and fruitless territory.

Daran Ajero had a way of making women behave irrationally. Look at the way she was thinking about him and behaving toward him. It was just the opposite of what she wanted to do. He had no trouble removing the nonchalant cloak she had donned for the evening. She couldn't remember when she had been so riled up—and so aroused. Why had it been so necessary for her to make sure that he knew how she felt about such issues? She wasn't sure, but she didn't like the importance he had assumed in her life. Their relationship had become one that she could not afford. Star had always believed in cutting quickly through the layers of confusion surrounding a problem and that often there was a simple solution waiting to be found. She decided that the solution in this case was to put distance and time between herself and Daran Ajero.

CHAPTER 7

After she told the support group about Daran and had gotten their support for her decision to keep her distance from him, Star couldn't believe how easy it had been to implement her plan. For an entire week she simply kept herself inaccessible to him. And out of sight was out of mind. Well, at least for a little while, or, at the very least, that's what she wanted him to think.

Since that night on the ferry, he called and left messages several times at both Gail's house and at the Placido. She simply had not returned his calls. She was not being cowardly, she told herself, she was just doing what had to be done. He was not the type of man who'd take no for an answer. If she didn't want a relationship with him, she'd have to show him she was not interested. The reality was that her previous strategy of going out with him to be neighborly and to show him she wasn't romantically interested had failed. Now she'd avoid him until she had a chance to get her balance back.

But convincing her sister of all this would be another matter. Star had decided to be direct with Gail. Nothing else would work anyway. Gail could read Star's feelings and thoughts so well that Star had learned a long time ago that if she wanted to keep something from her sister, she shouldn't even bring up the subject.

Was it just a coincidence that both Gail and Daran could detect her real feelings and thoughts so well, or was she just totally transparent? This thought crossed her mind as she turned into her sister's driveway. She had had a successful week of avoiding Mr. Daran Ajero. But she'd spent it at her condo, making up excuses for Gail and feeling guilty about abandoning her. Now here she was, on Saturday afternoon, back so close to his house she could almost feel him. She parked her car and dashed into the house, wanting to get away again as soon as possible.

She found her sister upstairs in her sewing and crafts room. This room was just off the long center hall, adjoining the master bedroom. If she was not downstairs or asleep in her bedroom, Gail could usually be found in this room—her studio, she called it—surrounded by all of her beloved fabrics, batting, designs, and all the other items that revealed her love of crafts.

When Star walked in, Gail could tell her sister had something on her mind. "Want to help me with this wall hanging?" she asked neutrally, holding up a multicolored assortment of squares dotted with tufts of yam.

"No, I wanted to talk to you about…It's, uh…Gail, I need to stay up at my place for a few more days." Star stole a look at her sister and saw a smile playing around Gail's mouth. Strolling to a bookshelf, Star fingered a book binding as she exclaimed, "I might as well tell you. Knowing you, you probably know more about what's going on than I do anyway!" Star took a deep breath. "It's about Daran and—"

"Oh, before you tell me, let me tell you what happened this afternoon. Cordelia came by looking for you." Not looking directly at her sister, Gail gave Star a chance to absorb this tidbit. "She gave me the update on her grand scheme to marry Daran. She figured you had told me about it, and of course I pretended that you had."

As Star opened her mouth to speak, Gail held up her hand. "Wait, let me finish. At first I wondered why you hadn't told me, but as she talked, I figured out why, sister dear. You've got a thing for this guy," Gail concluded with a mischievous grin.

"I wouldn't call it that."

"What would you call it? The hots?"

"Really, Gail, it's nothing like that. Besides, as you found out, it would be a waste of time for me to feel that way about him when that Cordelia is so dead set on marrying him. No doubt they spend every night between the sheets together."

"Well, actually, I didn't get that impression."

"Then your ferreting skills have become rusty, because if you consider the combined force of their libidos plus her plan, and let's not forget all those perfect opportunities they have…How can you even begin to think there's nothing happening?"

"Because she told me so."

Star's mouth fell open.

Gail laughed. "I got you there. Now pick your bottom lip up off the floor and sit down and listen." Star quickly moved toward one of the comfortable stuffed chairs as Gail continued talking.

"Cordy came over to see you this afternoon around two o'clock, and like I said, she assumed you'd told me about her plan. The woman is really quite a character!" Then noting Star's grimace of impatience, Gail continued, "She told me a man who adores her has come into her life." Gail batted her lashes coquettishly in an imitation of a woman in love. "She went on to say that she would've made a terrible mistake if she'd married Daran."

"Did Daran ask her to marry him or consent to marry her?"

"Oh, I did ask her about that. She called it just a matter of applying the right amount of pressure to precise points," Gail said, smiling, her voice laced with sarcasm. "I tell you, Star, the woman was so entertaining, I could have spent the whole afternoon with her."

Star thought swiftly. If Cordy was no longer interested in Daran, did her own reservations about a relationship with him still make sense? Was Cordy the only reason for her doubts? She had to answer no to that question, judging from the residue of fear that still remained. This was all so new. She needed time to mull it over, to put it aside and then bring it back and examine it again.

Gail noticed her sister's introspective expression and her voice was solemn. "Star, you look just like what Auntie Mellie always used to say about you, 'Those still waters sure run deep.' That Daran has gotten to you, girl. Not that I blame you. He's solid in every way; he has money to burn, and he's sure an attractive man."

"What makes you think he's interested in a serious relationship with me?"

"Oh, it probably has something to do with him asking me on a couple of occasions if you were seeing anybody, or maybe it's because he also wanted to know if you'd ever been hurt by a man. He's probably trying to account for your skittish behavior."

Star bristled, then stood up and paced. "I hope you didn't tell him anything more than you already had. That's totally sneaky—going to my sister to find out something he wouldn't have the nerve to ask me! You didn't tell him anything else, did you, Gail?"

Gail cupped her hand over her mouth in a "did I spill the beans?" expression. "Gail! Gail!" Star was speechless. She could only utter a sound that was part snort and part scream.

Gail twisted her mouth from side to side to prevent a spasm of giggles. Her composure regained, she said, "Star, I just told him that I didn't think there was anyone serious—nothing definite."

"Gee, thanks. Like you wouldn't know if I'm seeing somebody serious. You're only my sister. Gail, that's just why I didn't tell you anything that was going on. You meddle too much, sister dear.

You and he are just the same, meddlers. No wonder you get along so well."

Gail leaned forward in her chair, causing her patchwork to fall to the floor unnoticed. "Starmaine, I'm sorry if you think I'm meddling, but you're acting like an adolescent. You've also been licking your wounds from that Lance fiasco too long. That was two years ago. You've been punishing yourself for trusting him. You're supposed to trust. That's human. And you're supposed to learn from your mistakes. What's not right is for you to punish yourself. For goodness sakes, Star, don't let Lance poison your feelings toward every man. Didn't he hurt you enough already?"

"I know, I know. Next you'll remind me that you told me that he was no good."

"Only if I need to. Because he was no good for you, or any other woman for that matter, Starmaine. That's become clear."

Gail stopped. She took a deep breath and sighed. "Listen, Star, haven't you ever noticed how you keep me from going off the deep end and I do the same for you? I think we know each other better than we know ourselves."

Star shrugged. "Okay, Gail, I'll think about it. But what I wanted to tell you was that I need to spend a few more days at the condo. I have to do my monthly check-ins at the clubs in Chester and Upper Darby."

"No problem. You go ahead and get things sorted out, Star. I've got things under control here." Gail was silent for a moment. She picked her needlework up from the floor and then casually said, "Oh, I almost forgot. Cordy relayed an invitation from Daran asking us over to their place—or rather, his place—this evening. There's going to be a small dinner party. Very dressy. I told her we'd come."

Star could tell by the way Gail's eyes had fastened to her needlework that she dared not look up to see the reception this bombshell received.

"Great!" Star said with genuine enthusiasm. She laughed as Gail peeked out warily from behind the needlework she now held up to shield her face. Star watched her sister's expression shift from wariness to amazement.

"Well, I'll be darned," Gail said, "and I was expecting a great wall of resistance. Starmaine, there's no predicting you sometimes!"

"I can't wait to see the inside of that house. That's all." "You and me both!" Gail whooped, drumming her feet against the floor.

At six o'clock, Starmaine stood in front of the long mirror admiring her reflection. The red knit slide-off-the-shoulder dress gripped her wide shoulders snugly. Its surplice bodice molded to the curves of her breasts before trailing on down to subtly accentuate her hips and flare frivolously above her knees.

Reveling in Daran's anticipated reaction to her appearance, Star smiled seductively at her reflection before stepping into matching red pumps. She had to admit that tonight she was taking extra care with how she looked. Was she dressing for him? She wasn't sure. Up until now, he'd seen a very levelheaded side of her.

Tonight he'd see her playfulness. She was just in that kind of mood. And what if she did want him to look at her? A woman sometimes wanted and needed a man to look at her. She still hadn't decided if or how she would proceed with him beyond tonight. No decisions were necessary. She just wanted to be light-hearted and have fun—and even flirt with him. Ha! That would be a switch.

She knew she excited him, and damn it, she'd never been turned on as much by any other man. He stimulated her in ways and places that made her squirm even when she was away from him. Whereas many men bragged about their manly prowess, she was certain that he could deliver in the bedroom as surely as he succeeded in other endeavors. She'd be seeing him for the first time this evening on his own turf, in his castle, where he truly was king. Yet he acted as though he was in charge wherever he was. He was smooth and always moved about with such— what was the word? *Aplomb*. That was it.

How would she react to his overtures now that Cordy had flashed a green light? Had he demanded that she make it clear they weren't involved, or did the woman actually have a serious romantic interest in another man after so recently declaring her vow to snare Daran? How had that come about?

"Star, we'll be late," Gail shouted up the stairs.

"I've just fed Nan and I want to tuck her away in one of their upstairs bedrooms so she can go to sleep."

Giving herself a parting glance in the mirror, Star squirted a few drops of Je Reviens on strategic spots before turning with a flurry of skirt and leaving the room.

Gail emitted a shrill wolf whistle as she saw Star's long legs precede the rest of her body down the stairs. "Knock 'em dead red, girl! You're going to have steam fizzing out of every man there."

Star smiled, accepted the compliment, and admired Gail's elegant black sheath. As Gail chattered about the guest list and wondered aloud what the menu would be, Star busied herself locking the door behind them. She didn't tell her sister about the swarm of butterflies that hit her stomach. They fluttered there freely during the short drive to the grand house on the opposite side of the spoon.

She regretted wearing the slinky red dress as soon as she saw Cordy, who opened the door wearing full African regalia. Compared with Cordy's wholesome attire, her own dress felt provocative and cheap.

Amid warm greetings, the young African woman ushered them into a huge marble-floored foyer. A beautiful chandelier hung from a domed ceiling. The chandelier's bulbs were dimmed, gleaming like dying embers in the otherwise unlit area. A winding staircase at the foyer's end led to the upper rooms, whose doors opened onto a circular balcony. The balcony, with its polished wood railing, overlooked a large courtyard-style sunken living room off to the right of the foyer. Two large skylights let in the moonlight. It made the room's understated decor simply sumptuous.

"Let's take the baby upstairs and get her comfortable," Cordy prompted, and Gail followed her to the staircase, but not before raising her eyebrows at Star to show she was impressed. "Starmaine, go in and find the crowd," Cordy called over her shoulder.

Star could hear muted voices coming from somewhere inside the cavernous confines of the house. It seemed even bigger inside.

She stood still for long moments adjusting to the home's opulent interior. Maybe Daran's a crook, she thought, then nudged that thought aside with a more disturbing one about just what kind of crook he'd have to be to afford such a house and such a lifestyle.

"Cordelia, what's keeping you?" Star heard his voice as he moved toward her. Before she could move or make a sound, he entered the open space and stopped as he caught sight of her standing in the elevated foyer area. His eyes gave her a quick once-over and then did a slow crawl from her pump-encased feet to her side-swept hair. His nostrils flared and his eyelids jerked involuntarily. Then, breathing deeply, he moved toward her as she silently complimented him on the way his black suit and white shirt fell over the hard planes of his muscular physique.

"Starmaine, you're ravishing," he said, softly encasing her hand in his. Daran's face held no hint of his usual ready smile as his eyes caressed her hair, face, and neck and came to rest on her bare shoulders, which gave off a sheen even in the dimmed light. "Like so many of your sisters, at home and elsewhere, you have majestic shoulders. Dignified and delicate," he intoned. "I'm probably biased, but I think African women have the most beautiful shoulders in the world, shoulders that stand like reeds but move like a song. Of course many people think that their erect posture comes from carrying the little fat babies on their backs, but those who appreciate the wonders of nature know better. They know that the true beauty stems from the African woman's bone structure. Long, lithe limbs, elegant bones. Her carriage simply accentuates her architecture."

Despite the cool airiness of the spacious, two-story foyer, Star felt like she was suffocating. His light cologne mingled with his aura of masculinity and penetrated the space between them. She wanted him to go beyond the polite and expected. She fought these strong urges threatening to overwhelm her. They screamed at her to do something to quell the heavy waves of excitement that swept her very core. Her eyelids fluttered shut for a split second as she battled the intensity of her feelings. Clenching her teeth, she concluded: wrong time, wrong place, but right man.

Of that much she was certain. Maybe other certainties would reveal themselves. It was like crossing out all the wrong choices on a multiple-choice test until you found the best answer. Her mind raced ahead, posing all sorts of questions and answers about him. What would his kisses be like? Deep and wet, soft and gentle, or urgent and demanding? How would his body move against hers? Slow and stroking, hard and unyielding, wild and abandoned, or rough but controlled? What sounds would he make? Whispers and moans, growls and groans, gasps and sighs, or concentrated silence?

She shoved aside these lascivious thoughts and got control of herself before he'd read the raw emotions on her features. What she had in mind was certainly not suited to the foyer, not when dinner guests were waiting for the host to return.

She smiled coquettishly. "You're looking great yourself," she said, allowing him to caress her hand as she slipped into her role as the outrageous flirt. It was as good a cover as any, and without some protection, she'd be completely lost in him.

Busily scanning her face, his alert eyes detected the hint of strain that hovered over her features. A puzzled expression crossed his face before he arched an eyebrow at her. An amused glint twinkled in his eyes. She lifted her head, and knowing she looked as good as he made her feel, she put her hand in the crook of his elbow and prodded him to move in the direction of his guests.

His dinner guests consisted of a Senegalese doctor and his young wife, a vice-president of a Nigerian bank and his protégé, and a wealthy West African oil minister and his African American wife, who became keenly interested in Starmaine when she found out about Star's work as a fitness consultant. Apparently the woman, a Mrs. Akala, was giving a lot of thought to setting up a luxurious health resort in one of the continent's glittering spots. "I'll keep in touch with you, dear. I'm sure we can do some business." Starmaine assured her this was entirely possible.

During a dinner of squab with scallion stuffing and fresh green peas, served by uniformed servants hired for the occasion, Gail and Cordy sat opposite each other at the gleaming black lacquer table. At the rectangular table's end and near Star sat Daran who was opposite Mrs. Akala at the other end. Mr. Akala sat on the far side of Cordy near his wife, while Cordy's beau Max sat between Star and Cordy. The young doctor, his wife, Gail, and Godfrey, the banker, sat on the other side of the table.

The conversation was jovial, with Godfrey and Daran trading humorous anecdotes about their experiences traveling to many of the world's large cities. As Star expected, Daran was the consummate host, very attentive to even the smallest detail and anticipating his guests' needs and wants. Whenever she looked at him directly, Daran's wine-brown eyes sparkled as they gazed at her. Even when he wasn't returning her look, however, she was keenly aware that he was aware of her. His darting glances and intimate smiles took care of that and only encouraged the restless energy that surged through her.

After dessert and coffee, the guests adjourned to the great room, a room that served as a media center as well as an all-purpose recreation room. Along with the latest media equipment built into one wall, the room boasted. a huge stone fireplace, a wet bar, several seating areas, and a glass wall overlooking a portion of the top level of the two-tiered terrace.

As Godfrey and the young doctor squared off for a game of billiards and Gail became engaged in an earnest conversation with Mrs. Akala and the doctor's wife about what life was like in Africa, Cordy and Max sat away from the rest, talking softly. Though Starmaine was extremely curious about Cordy's adoring suitor and the whirlwind change of Cordy's mind, she didn't want to make herself obvious. She kept her distance by walking along one section of the brick wall near the fireplace, admiring the striking African art that lined the wall and shelves. She could feel Daran's eyes on her, even as he seemed to be paying close attention to the game the men were playing. Once when she glanced in his direction, he turned at that exact moment and their eyes met, erasing the distance between them. Minutes later, he moved toward her.

"I've been the polite host to them long enough," he said softly as he came up behind her.

"You haven't exactly been attentive to me since we left the dining room. I declare, I feel neglected," she teased, turning toward him. "Are you trying to ignore me?"

"No man with a pulse could ignore you, Starmaine. Godfrey has been undressing you all night. And if I were any more attentive to you, it wouldn't be decent," he said into her ear, so close and so intimate that the fervor of his tone caused the flood of restless energy to streak wildly through her again. A momentary scant frown flickered across her features as she fought its debilitating effects. She averted her gaze from his but not soon enough.

"Are you all right?" "Sure. It's nothing. I must be tired. I'm an early riser."

"Oh, then I must find some way to stimulate you, to keep you awake. A good host always aims to please."

She darted a glance at him to determine the intent of his remarks that sounded so laden with innuendos.

"Come, let me show you the rest of the house and we'll look in on your niece," he said loudly enough for the others to hear. Gail flashed a smile at them as they left the room.

As soon as they got out of sight of the others, Daran grasped her hand and entwined his arm in hers. "I've been wanting to touch you all evening," he said as he pulled her up a short flight of stairs that led through an octagonal-shaped kitchen and then down a few steps into a darkened corridor.

"Starmaine, I've got to touch you. I mean, really touch you," he said, pressing her back against a wall as his mouth sought hers in the darkness. Their lips locked hungrily and his tongue invaded her mouth, frantically grasping and seeking, unable to savor what he found, so great was the sheer pleasure of the physical contact. Starmaine gave herself up to the moment and to the rampage on her senses. The hunger that she had felt all evening took control of the lower half of her body, causing her to move her hips in an undulating motion against his hard body as he kneed her legs apart and moved against her. She gasped as she felt the hardness and heat of his masculinity pressing against her through the thin cotton knit of her dress. Never before had she felt so exposed.

"Starmaine, you feel so good," he muttered, moving against her as his lips and teeth nibbled at her ears, neck, and bare shoulders.

"Please, Starmaine, let me..." he panted. "Let me..." One hand went under her dress and slid up the back of her legs, where it palmed her derriere, pulling her into his middle. A moment later, his other hand was tugging at the waistband of her pantyhose.

I've got to stop this, she said to herself, even though his hands were everywhere and the incessant friction brought her closer and closer to the sweet release she hungered for.

"We can't," she murmured, and made a feeble attempt to draw away.

"We're not doing anything yet," he murmured, plundering her mouth once again with hard kisses and pulling at the waistband of her hose. His other hand slid back and forth across her derriere, dizzying her, driving her ever closer to a threshold.

"Can't," she whispered. "Suppose someone comes in here and catches us like this?" Even as she said the words, she cringed, knowing he would interpret them as the go-ahead to continue his delicious marauding of her flesh, her mind, her senses. And she'd be a hypocrite to say she didn't want him. No, they had gone too far to deny the intense craving, the thunderous passion he aroused in her. But an even stronger emotion gripped her, and good sense began to seep past the ache his mouth and hands had created. She didn't want cheap thrills in a darkened hallway. She didn't know precisely what else she wanted, but it was a far cry from that. With that sure knowledge, she stood stock-still and tensed her body, and by the decreased pace of his roving hands a split second later, she knew that he sensed her changed mood.

"We've got to stop this now," she said, hardening her voice, to give her tone the conviction her body did not feel.

"Please don't say that," he hissed in a voice hoarse with desire. With determination, she brought her hands down from his muscular shoulders. She grasped his hands.

He held her tightly for a few seconds longer before releasing her and stepping back from her. "You're right," he said as he sought to bring his breathing under control again. "The time is not right. Let's go." He found her hand in the dark and led her back.

During the brief walk, Star realized that their relationship was now cast in a new light. It had changed, and she wondered whether for the better or worse. The old fears and doubts lingered. Gail was right. The truth was, she was afraid of a relationship with Daran because of Lance. Despite the temptation, she resolved yet again never to let a man treat her as Lance had.

Moments after leaving the storage room and walking down a short corridor, Daran opened double wood-paneled doors to a library. Full bookshelves were set into the walls of the room. It was a magnificent room filled with the warmth of rich wood and plants and books.

"My favorite room in the house," he said, glancing around and then turning his gaze to her. "I love to read, Starmaine. I read for knowledge; I read for stimulation; and I read for pleasure. That's another thing that you now know about me," he said as the familiar smile returned to his face and his eyes rested on her.

Starmaine decided that the moment was as good a time as any to put what had happened into perspective. "Daran, I'm...I'm..." She pressed her hand to her forehead, unable to find the words she sought.

He took her by the shoulders and turned her to face him. "You're what, Starmaine? Bothered by the fact that I touched you or that you responded?"

"I should never have let you touch me like that. I don't know what happened to me. I'm not like that usually. You must think—"

"I think that you're very passionate and an extremely desirable woman who I would've given anything to have in my bed a few minutes ago. And don't forget, you were touching me, too."

Starmaine tried to pull away from him, still unable to handle what had happened. "No matter what you say, you must think I'm cheap." There, she said it, the word she so hated.

"No, Starmaine. That's what you're thinking." He stopped and sighed deeply. "Look, it's simple. You did something you wanted to do. You have needs and you responded to me in a way that's natural. Starmaine, you must know that I care for you. But there's a part of you that persists in seeing me as a guy who's out to just have some quick fun with you. I'm not like that. I'm not a teenage boy who's trying to score, nor am I the type of man who thinks that all a woman has to offer is between her legs. Just face it. For a few moments, you were a woman without artifice, just pure emotion, pure passion. I made you feel good and natural. You liked it. That's normal. That's what makes the world go round."

"And what about you? How did you feel? Rewarded for your hot pursuit?"

"Oh, I could've felt better," he said, refusing to take the sting of her snide remark. Instead he smiled fully and winked at her. "A lot better. But tonight I'm with a special woman, and at times like this, a man has to take a rain check if he doesn't want to ruin his chances with her."

He cupped her chin with his hand and pulled her lips apart, staring at the slight openness for a moment before his wine-brown eyes slid up to blaze into hers. Starmaine had the sudden sensation that he was branding her with his eyes as his hot fingers had branded her only moments before.

During the next days, Star's job schedule kept her so busy that she fell into bed at night and slept a dreamless sleep. She could keep her body busy, but even in her busiest moments, she did not totally succeed at blotting out the memory of Daran. Snatches of his voice, expressions, mannerisms, or smile would parade through her mind without any invitation. It was as if he were there—pervasive and persistent, brashly and imperiously telling her what he wanted from her in unequivocal terms. Her only consolation was that he wasn't really there to see how easily she capitulated to his demands. She knew he was away on business in Atlanta, so even if she'd been sure she wanted to, she couldn't see him.

She and Gail talked every day on the phone: she called her sister at the school during Gail's lunch period or at home in the evening, more often the latter, but sometimes at both places. Star knew that her actual motivation for the evening calls was to determine whether Daran had left a message for her on Gail's answering machine, and by midweek, Gail knew too.

"No, Star. Daran did not call," Gail said as soon as she heard Star's voice.

"Really, Gail, if he wanted to call me, he could reach me here at the condo. I'm listed in the white pages. Or he could call me at the Placido. Atlanta is probably keeping him all too busy. That's not why I'm ca—"

"Did you ever even tell the man your last name?"

"Believe me, if a man as resourceful as Daran wanted to get in touch with me, he would find a way. Atlanta is not Pago Pago. I'm sure he's not having a problem getting a call through."

Star felt a little miffed and, yes, neglected. She was annoyed at herself for these feelings. He had succeeded in doing what she'd tried to prevent; he'd gotten into her thoughts. And her heart? She'd tried hard to keep him from mattering to her so that if he proved insincere, it wouldn't bother her. He had apparently done what she'd only struggled to do; he had put her out of his mind, just as Lance had when another woman caught his attention. She realized now that she'd been kidding herself all along about Daran; clearly, he mattered a great deal to her.

"Thanks, Daran Ajero, for teaching me a lesson before I became totally duped again," she said aloud to the empty condo. "Fool me once, shame on you. Fool me twice…"

The giant jumbo jet took off from the bustling West African airport with a roar. Daran sat with his head back against the comfortable seat's headrest. He wasn't even aware when the plane leveled off or when the other passengers began to unfasten their seat belts and move around.

Starmaine was on his mind. As a matter of fact, ever since that first day on the porch, the memory of how she looked, smelled, tasted, and felt had been branded on his brain. There'd also been a tension in his body that he didn't want to relieve with other women even though there were numerous opportunities in both Atlanta and the various African cities his business had called him to during the two weeks following the dinner party. He'd held himself in check admirably that night on the ferryboat too, he thought. No matter how great his need to hold her soft, wondrous curves next to him, he knew that the intensity of his feelings for her might scare her off. It was easily detectable that she'd been badly hurt—just as he had. Once in a lifetime was enough, thank you. And he hadn't even considered getting serious about a woman before he met her, not after the disaster with Elaine.

After his divorce, his uncle had told him that there would come a time when he'd find another woman he could care for because "that's the culture and that's life." When his uncle had seen the spark of protest in his eyes, the old man wagged a finger and flung an old African proverb at him: "You listen to your elders because 'you may have a new suit of clothes, but you'll never have as many rags as your father.' "

On this trip he visited his uncle briefly. The old man was sickly, but somehow he knew that Daran had found a woman. He grinned at his nephew. "You look like a man who feels a woman, but you don't know if she feels you yet. Go and make her feel you and have many *pekins*," the old man advised, using the broken English word for children.

Daran visited his mother, too. Knowing she had been lonely since his father had died years before, he always made a special effort to visit when he could. This time she too seemed to know about Starmaine. Although he had come unexpectedly, she had given him a packet of jewelry that contained two matching sets of ornately carved gold necklaces, earrings, bracelets, and rings. Though it had been a while since his mother had been actively involved in gold trading, he knew that she still kept in contact with the region's African Women's Gold Consortium. Sure enough, the letters AWGC were faintly inscribed on each piece of jewelry.

"Give the bracelet to your wife-to-be when you propose to her. Give her the necklace when she consents to marry our family and give her the remaining pieces on the day she marries you. Give the other set to your wife's mother on the day of the wedding. That way her family will think favorably of our family and they will help to quell any arguments that might arise between you and your wife."

He had thanked his mother. As he placed the valuable packet in his briefcase, she'd added, "Daran, this wife must learn our ways."

"Yes, Mother," he said, speaking to her in their native tongue as she always spoke to him.

As he unwrapped the jewelry now to touch it, he wondered how Starmaine would react when he presented it to her. That is, if he ever got the chance to present it to her. He would have to go slowly, and it certainly wouldn't hurt to ask an orisha—one of the deities—to give him some help.

In the meantime, he figured he might as well finish the feasibility report he'd been requisitioned to do for the Atlanta plastics company. They wanted to set up a branch of their company in the Ivory Coast and they wanted to do it immediately, if it were feasible. He'd stumbled on this piece of business during what he thought was to be a three-day business trip to Atlanta. Instead, he had had to go to the Ivory Coast, where it had taken nearly two weeks to obtain the information he needed for the report. It would have taken him even longer if it hadn't been for his invaluable contacts in the region. Thanks to heaven and earth.

The plastics company was paying him an astronomical fee for his services, and no doubt the anxious New York executives would have their messenger at the airport waiting for his report. With this in mind, he pulled out his laptop computer and began to write. It would be ten hours before the plane touched down at Kennedy Airport, but once the report was out of his hands, he'd rent a car and drive as fast as he could home to Delaware, to Starmaine.

For once, he wished he could just head straight to Delaware without having to hang around New York at all. He wanted to be near her. He needed to be near her. She was the kind of woman that made a man's hard work worthwhile. Just the thought of having her to come home to after these trips was as revitalizing as finding water in a desert—and abundantly more pleasurable. There were all kinds of thirsts and hungers, some that could only be satisfied by one woman's touch. The thought of that happening caused everything to shift out of focus for a dizzying moment. A fine sheen of perspiration broke out over his body.

Moments later, still reeling from the intensity of the feeling, Daran shook his head hard a few times to clear his mind. If he was to get any work done, he couldn't start thinking about her now. A strong dose of willpower enabled him to push Starmaine from his mind, and his fingers moved rapidly over the computer keyboard.

Two hours later, he finished the report, and as he leaned his head back against the seat, the gentle vibrations of the jet moving westward rocked him to sleep.

At the same time that Daran was drifting off to sleep on the plane, Star was lifting the phone to call Rex. His private phone, a separate one, at his mother's house rang four times before his answering machine responded. She left a message confirming their plans to drive down to do some sightseeing in Cape May, New Jersey, the next day, Friday

"Let's leave around ten A.M. so we can get there in time to have a leisurely lunch in one of those quaint inns," she said.

But the next morning, Rex did not arrive until eleven-fifteen. He apologized for being late, explaining that his daughter was sick and he wasn't sure it was fair to leave his mother alone with her. But when the little girl had perked up some, he had decided it would be all right and had come ahead after all.

They lost more time stopping at a service station, and then later stopping again, this time for food. By the time they finally reached Cape May it was a little after three that afternoon. By then they were both ravenous again, so after a leisurely meal, they hurriedly did some touring of the small town.

About six, after they had located a beautifully maintained Victorian bed-and-breakfast to stay in overnight, Rex called home to check on his daughter. The worried look on his face when he returned to the car indicated that the day would not have a happy ending. His words confirmed this. His daughter's temperature had risen and his mother was preparing to take the child to the hospital. He had to leave.

Star pointed out that they could make the trip back faster by putting the car on the ferry to Windy Bay. That way they'd avoid all the late afternoon up-coast New Jersey traffic. Once the ferry landed at Windy Bay, they could take the relatively unclogged Delaware interstate highway back up to Philly.

The ferry ride was uneventful, but no sooner had they left the ferryboat than rain began to pour down in sheets. "Oh damn!" Rex said. "I heard on the weather report yesterday there was a chance a bad storm would hit the coast. I figured it was worth a chance, Star, because I knew how you'd been wanting to stay overnight in a bed-and-breakfast. I thought it could be a beginning for us," Rex said apologetically.

"It's okay, Rex. I just want you to get back to your daughter," she said tersely, wanting to kick herself for not checking the weather report herself.

The storm-darkened twilight coupled with the heavy rain made the visibility so poor that they were forced to virtually creep along the deserted roads of the beach town. In no time the roads were flooded and after the car swam through a deep puddle, it sputtered and came to a stop.

"Now what?" Rex muttered, banging the steering wheel with a clenched fist.

It took a few seconds before Star thought of Tiger, Daran's restaurant-owning friend. He was the only person she knew in Windy Bay. Peering through the murky grayness, she spotted a phone booth a few feet from where they sat in the dark car.

She rummaged in her bag for coins, pulled her jacket over her head, and dashed for the phone, hoping fervently that it was working.

By nine-thirty, the worst of the storm had passed. Tiger had truly been a godsend. He rushed over from the restaurant with a tow hook and chain and had towed Rex's ailing vehicle to a local garage before dropping Rex at the local Amtrak train station. When Rex protested again about leaving Star behind, she said, "Just go to your daughter. I'll drive the car up tomorrow."

Now that she and Tiger were alone, she saw the questions were still on his face, questions about Rex, but she still refused to acknowledge them. She simply introduced Rex as a co-worker and left it at that. Tiger took Star to his restaurant to eat. After she finished another delicious meal, he told her she could stay overnight at a friend's house.

Star didn't realize until he opened the door to the two-story beach dwelling that it was vacant. And it had the smell of being rarely used. She was too exhausted to ask questions, however, and after being assured by Tiger that the house was specially built to withstand major storms, she peeled off her still-damp clothes and luxuriated in a warm bath before climbing into the king-sized bed in one of the bedrooms. Moments later, she drifted asleep.

CHAPTER 8

After calling several places Cordelia had suggested, to no avail, Tiger finally tracked Daran down in Dover at the home of a professor who taught at the local college.

When the phone rang, Daran was vigorously engaged in an ancient African board game called Wari. The professor was an avid player of the game. Daran had just strategically distributed his pebbles along the elaborately carved oblong board when the jangling ring of the nearby phone intruded.

"It's someone named Tiger, for you," the professor said, after absentmindedly lifting the receiver and speaking into it. His mind returned to the game even before Daran's hand took the phone.

As Daran thrust the receiver to his ear, his heart pounded. Nothing short of an emergency would prompt Tiger to seek him out here.

"Ki'l owo?" Daran said, switching to his native language.

After Tiger had described the reason for the call, Daran assured him that it was perfectly all right for Starmaine to stay at his beach house. Actually Daran couldn't think of anything he relished more. But a ripple of jealousy coursed through him when Tiger had mentioned that Starmaine had originally planned to stay overnight at a bed-and-breakfast with a male friend. Tiger told him he had dropped the gentleman off at the station to get the train back to Philadelphia. He wondered if it was the mannequin from the restaurant. Bed-and-breakfast, be damned! He could just imagine the night of ecstasy that guy had in mind. All bed and too exhausted for breakfast was more like it!

Of course Daran wouldn't voice these sentiments to Tiger, but his friend must have intuited them because he chuckled and said, "I didn't think you would mind since she is alone, but I just wanted to check."

Daran replaced the receiver in its cradle and sat down opposite the professor. He glanced at the game board, but the stark reality of the situation between him and Starmaine made it impossible to concentrate on the fate of pebbles. There was so much between them that was unresolved. The reality of the situation was that he loved her. There! He said it.

Starmaine was never far from his thoughts these days. He saw her creamy brown skin in his milk-laced tea. The sunshine reminded him of the way her smile outshone the brightest surroundings. The sleek, lithe movements of her divine figure made him twitch. And when he was near her, every nerve in his body stood at full attention.

They needed some undistracted time to talk, man to woman. He suddenly wanted to tell her that he loved her, that she had had an effect on him he'd never thought possible, that around her he registered just a hair short of being out of control, that he wanted to marry her and spend the future with her.

How she would respond, he didn't know, but he would persist. He'd find a way to have her.

Have her? He suddenly wondered how much his behavior around her had to do with the fact that he had not been with a woman for over a year. Was it pure, unadulterated sex that he craved? Was it the fact that she had brought him out of the cave of abstinence he had dwelled in since the revelations about Elaine? Plenty of women had tried to get him interested during the past year—including Cordelia—but they hadn't succeeded. No, he wasn't at the mercy of his hormones. Sure, he wanted to luxuriate in the soft, hot moistness of her flesh, but that wasn't all.

Nonetheless, the images that swam before his eyes of their bodies meshing made his hands tremble.

"Some upsetting news, Daran?" The professor's words and the puzzled expression on the older man's face brought Daran out of his reverie.

"No, actually, it's good news, I hope," Daran said, rising and making up his mind. "I need to attend to it right away, though, if you don't mind me leaving so abruptly."

"Not at all. I can tell that your mind is not in this room." He escorted Daran to the door. "Be careful on those wet roads tonight," the professor cautioned.

Moments later, Daran gunned the motor of his car, and within minutes he was on the southbound highway on his way to a long-overdue encounter with Starmaine.

Just knowing that she was somewhere in the confines of his beach house alone almost drove him to distraction during the forty-five-minute drive to Windy Bay. His hands clutched the steering wheel, his viselike grip a poor attempt to control his anticipatory tremor.

"Damn you, Starmaine!" he swore as he noted that the speedometer hovered around ninety several times before he forced himself to slow down.

Finally he rolled down the window and tried to think about calmer subjects as the dark, storm-soaked Delaware countryside floated past the car.

A conversation he'd had with Cordelia just before leaving home entered his mind. She mentioned that Max Akimaba had asked her to accompany him on a visit to a relative. Daran smiled, remembering Max's attempts after the Atlanta meeting to find out the nature of Daran's relationship with Cordelia.

After giving Max a short history of the close connection between his and Cordelia's family, he'd told Max directly that no romantic relationship of any sort had ever existed or ever been considered by him. Knowing the cultural condemnation that a man who touched a woman entrusted to his care by her family would face was assurance enough for Max that Daran spoke the truth. The soft-spoken, mild-mannered man's face had split into a broad grin before he became serious again and asked Daran for permission to befriend Cordelia.

Daran had remarked, "She's a woman and she's old enough and you are a decent man and a wealthy one, I might add, so why not?"

Apparently the quiet little man was in hot pursuit now. Daran didn't know what amazed him more, Max's interest in the willful and unpredictable

Cordelia or hers in a man who was a quiet and humorless businessman. Daran sincerely hoped that Cordelia was interested in more than just the man's money.

Daran arrived in Windy Bay around eleven and five minutes later stood at the bottom of the beach house staircase. He found himself feeling nervous outside his own house. A glimmer of light, apparently from the main bathroom on the second floor, dimly lit the second floor hallway. He put his key in the lock of the dark beach house and entered without a sound. Flipping on a recessed light above the foyer's half-wall, he noted that except for a black umbrella in the umbrella stand, the room looked as tidy and cozy as usual. He could, however, detect a faint fragrance in the air. It was a familiar one—the light scent of fresh-cut flowers and lemon—the perfume that Starmaine wore.

Daran tiptoed up the stairs, being most careful not to make them creak. Should he make some noise to let her know of his presence? Should she be given some warning so she wouldn't be afraid?

In the end, he decided a noise would frighten her if she was asleep, as the silence of the house suggested. He wondered which of the two bedrooms she had chosen, but as he reached the second-floor landing, he could hear soft breathing coming from the larger bedroom, the one he always used.

As he passed the illuminated main bathroom, he saw a pair of wet bikini panties hanging over the shower rod. The scent of her perfume hung in the air and permeated the entire floor.

Glancing through the darkened bedroom's wide-open door, he saw a small suitcase next to the armoire and remembered that Tiger had said an overnight trip to Cape May had been planned. As his eyes adjusted to the darkness of the bedroom, he took in her form: she lay on her left side, her knees bent slightly. The sheet across her rose and fell with her breathing, but it was the way that the sheet clung to the contours of her body that told him she was naked underneath it.

The thought of her lying naked in his bed excited him immensely, and for a moment he was riveted to the spot by desire. Suddenly she stirred. He thought she would surely jolt awake and see him staring at her, but she turned so that she lay flat on her back, one leg bent at an angle. As she moved, the sheet came off her body. He was transfixed by the beauty of her caramel-eolored curves. But it was the darkened aureole of her breast coupled with the dark triangular patch at the pit of her belly that started such a trembling in him that he forced himself toward the other bedroom.

As Daran shed his clothes in the second bedroom, he became aware of the tautness of his muscles. He was kidding himself if he thought he could sleep that night with her just a few feet away. He quickly pulled his clothes back on, then shed them again and headed for the shower.

He'd make it an icy one.

Daran very carefully removed Star's bikini-cut panties from the shower rod, relishing the feel of the soft, filmy material as he did so. He held them in his hand for a long moment, rolling them between his fingers, then crushed them and smothered his face in them. Her soft lacy panties held the light fragrance she usually wore mixed in with her distinctly female aroma. This intoxicating mixture set off a dizzying sensation in him that made him hurriedly turn on the shower and step into its cool spray. For long moments, the streams of cold water pummeled his hot and tortured body. Finally as he felt the coldness lessen some of the tension, he began to hum a tune he'd learned as a little boy in Africa. Then he recalled the words to the song and began to sing them. His deep voice echoed in the large bathroom and carried throughout the house.

In a dream Starmaine heard a man singing. His voice was very familiar and made her feel warm and comforted. She loved the sound of the voice and knew whose voice it was, but in true dreamlike fashion, she could not find the man. The voice became louder and louder and she smiled as she searched in a field looking for this singing man who played hide-and-go-seek with her.

The cessation of the shower spray brought Starmaine awake; the man still hummed the tune. She sat up in the bed, pulling the sheet up over her naked breasts as she became aware of her surroundings and remembered the situation she was in. Suddenly terri-fied, she wondered whether the man was Tiger. When he had dropped her off at this place, he said he would speak to her the next day. Had he slipped back for some unsavory purpose?

Her terror mounting tenfold by the second, Star peered around in the dark, trying to find her clothes. The man began to sing the lyrics of the song again, and through her fog of fear, Star suddenly recognized Daran's voice!

Daran Ajero here in this house, and there she lay, as bare as a plucked chicken! Just as she began to make a move for her blouse and slacks, she saw his shadow hit the wall opposite the brightly lit bathroom. From his silhouette, she could tell that he was wrapping a towel around his lower body.

Then before she had time to react, he stood in the doorway of the bedroom, his eyes adjusting to the darkened room. "Hello, Starmaine. I hope I didn't scare you," he said softly.

She sat on the edge of the bed, one foot on the floor and the other one underneath her. She felt a mixture of surprise and relief that it was Daran, and was also titillated by knowing that he was as bare beneath the towel as she was beneath the sheet.

"Oh, yeah, I did have a few mind-bending moments of terror until I recognized your voice." She shook her head to clear it. "How did you get in here? Why are you here?"

"This is my house, Starmaine," he said softly, pausing to give her time to digest that tidbit of information. "And, as for why I'm here, Tiger called me and told me that he brought you here after some car trouble you had." He paused.

"I couldn't miss this opportunity to see you, Starmaine," he added softly "Does seeing me disappoint you? Or would you prefer it if I were someone else?" he asked as he moved slowly, mesmerizingly toward her in the darkened room.

He sat down near her on the bed, and although she didn't look directly at him, she could feel his eyes on her. Her nostrils flared as millions of pinpoints of heat pricked her body. It became a struggle to breathe.

"I want to make love to you, Starmaine," he whispered in a voice raw with desire. "I want to make love to you so badly." His tone, though ragged with emotion, had a lulling, caressing quality.

The tension in the room was palpable. Star turned away from him and inhaled deeply. She squeezed her eyes shut and dug her nails into her palms as she fought her own tormenting emotions. She wanted this man with every fiber of her body, but even though Cordy had other interests now, there were still reasons why it could be a mistake.

"A mistake, Daran," she muttered. "It would be a mistake." She held herself still, statue-like, her voice ringing hollow and flat while her emotions clamored, twisted, and raged.

He rose from the bed and kneeled before her. Cupping her chin, he turned her face toward him. "Look at me and listen to me, Starmaine," he ordered. "It will not be a mistake. I promise you that." He brought her right hand to his face and rubbed the back of it slowly across his cheek and around to his parted lips. He kissed, sucked, and nipped at each of her fingers before moving on to her palm.

Star shivered and tried to withdraw her hand from his feverishly hot lips. However, he refused to release it now that she had allowed him that tiny liberty.

"Relax, Starmaine," he whispered as his kisses began moving up her arm. "Give this night to us, just to be together, to touch each other, to hold each other. We've both wanted this for so long."

Starmaine lay back slightly, not realizing that the sheet had slid down from her breasts until she heard his intake of breath. She opened her eyes and looked to where his eyes had fastened on her breasts. Her nipples were taut and she felt a tingling fire threaten to spread between her thighs.

"Ahhh," he groaned hoarsely. His hot breath seared her flesh. "Starmaine, you're magnificent. You're so damn beautiful, so magnificently beautiful."

She heard his voice change from gravel to fur, from huskiness to whispers. She could smell their pent-up longing for each other. It wafted in the air, mingling with and simultaneously overriding their expensive store-bought fragrances. A gushing stream of blatant sensuality oozed in the darkened room, causing sensations of sheer abandon to overwhelm her. She wanted him so badly, so totally, that she felt she would explode into nothingness if he didn't touch her that instant.

She moaned then, a sound of surrender, the capitulation he needed to hear before going further.

Before the sound was finished, his eager mouth explored one of her throbbing nipples. With the tip of his tongue, he teased, licked, and then rolled each nipple between his lips. The exquisite pleasure that his teasing, tugging tongue and lips gave each nipple was so intense that Starmaine began to moan and squirm uncontrollably. Her arms encircled his head. She pulled him to her, smothering his face in her soft flesh as he continued his tender assault on her senses.

With his hands, he feather-stroked her sides slowly and rhythmically from her waist up to her breasts. His lips and flitting tongue were hot and wet as they strayed from her breasts, giving equal attention to every square inch of her torso. As his lips trailed to her lower belly, Star crested a dizzying threshold. He had taken her to the top of a cliff and now she wanted to float down.

Needing him to spread his touch to other parts of her, she wanted him on her, in her, fast. She lay back on the bed and spread her legs wide to receive him as she pulled him toward her. He did not follow her lead.

Puzzled by his resistance, she opened her eyes and saw him standing over her. The towel had dropped from his waist and a glance below his waist made her gasp. He jutted out long and thick.

"Come here, Starmaine," he whispered.

She hesitated only for a moment. Almost in a trance, she got up on her knees and moved to the edge of the bed. He took her hand and guided it to his steely hardness. As soon as she touched him, he hissed loudly and Star felt the tremors coursing through his body.

Being careful not to dislodge her hand, he lowered himself to the bed. "Don't turn me loose, my darling—just hold me like that." As he talked, they eased themselves down on their sides facing each other.

"Oh Starmaine! This is such sweet torture! But I knew from the first, that day on the porch when my lips touched your flesh, that you were what I needed. I needed you to complete my life. That touch branded me." He chuckled. "That's why it almost killed me to face the fact that you were Larry's wife, to know that I could never touch you again or have you touch me like this. It was torture to lie in my bed at night knowing that you were off-limits! Larry's wife!"

Star could no longer lie still next to him. His voice and words excited her beyond reason, sending her on a spiraling course of desire. Keeping her hand wrapped around his rock-hard center, she needed no further coaching and his head arched back on the bed as she straddled him and caressed his length and satiny tip with both hands.

Lying back on the bed and looking up at this beauty whose ministrations gave him such unbridled pleasure, he clenched his teeth and summoned up all his control not to explode in her hands. He slowly, lightly kneaded the sides of her thighs. She began to moan softly. His right hand moved around one thigh through her mass of tangled curls until he found what he sought. Her body came down closer to his as he stroked. She began to moan his name loudly as he continued to reciprocate the pleasure that she gave him.

"Starmaine, I don't have anything with me," he rasped. She heard his voice through the haze of pleasure that shrouded her. She heard what he said, but she didn't want his words to be true, so she refused to process them. They had no meaning. She had transcended a world where words were necessary. Her excitement and need were so great that her brain didn't function normally. She could not accept the words.

Abruptly, he grabbed her fondling hands that with each caress weakened his ability to say what had to be said or do what had to be done.

"Starmaine, dearest. I don't have a condom! And the town is shut down because of the storm."

Her head snapped up. "Damn you!" she shrieked through clenched teeth. Her body shook as she sobbed. "How can you get me to this point and not be prepared!"

He lowered her onto the bed next to him as he talked to her soothingly, "Listen to me, Starmaine. I don't want us to take foolish chances that you'll regret later. I'm healthy, but you don't know that. You'll wonder about that tomorrow and you'll be scared that you're pregnant or worse. You'll despise me and call me a selfish man, and you'll hate yourself for taking dangerous chances. And you won't want me to get near you, and that'll make me have to work even harder. We can wait, Starmaine, I want more than one night. Realize that. That's what I've been trying to get through to you. I love you, Starmaine, and I want us to start off the right way, with no regrets."

After a long disappointing moment, Star realized what good sense he made and she appreciated him all the more. After she'd gotten over her initial disappointment, she was happy to know that he had the control and wisdom to see beyond the night. She knew she would have regretted such a casual, unprotected encounter. He wasn't a short-term grabber, as were so many men; he was a long-range planner. He said he loved her. That was music to her ears, but she didn't know quite how she felt about him. There was still that fear inside her—that love opened the door to pain, humiliation, and more pain. But she knew she could trust him; she felt with him—this moment she did. And she trusted herself in feeling this. He had her best interests at heart. His judgment was like a security blanket that would not be blown off even in the fiercest wind.

"Besides," he whispered, touching her breast lightly, "there are other ways. I can give you as much pleasure tonight as you can handle without us taking foolish chances."

His touch caused a new wave of heat to leap through her body. She lay there for a moment, marveling at what his hands could make her feel. Then she rolled a few feet from him in the large bed and put her back to him.

"Like you said, Daran, I'm a woman and you're a man and there's only so much we can withstand before we answer nature's call."

He chortled. "I'm impressed that you remember what I said to you. Hmm, that must have been almost two weeks ago. It means that you've been thinking about me," and Star could tell that he was only half teasing. He was fishing—trying to find out how she felt about him. When she knew for sure, she'd let him know.

He paused to give to her a chance to respond, but she did not. Away from his hands, if not out of his bed, her reservations began to loom again. She held him in high esteem for not taking advantage of her in a passionate moment. Was she afraid of what Larry might think? She dismissed this thought as soon as it arose. She was an adult, after all. What could Larry or anyone else say?

Daran put his hand on her shoulder and gently tried to pull her flat on her back, but she would not budge. "What are you thinking, Starmaine? You're withdrawing from me again. I can feel the wall go up. If you're still worrying about Cordy and me, forget it. Cordy is involved." He laughed. "She barely knows I'm alive these days."

"Daran, it's not Cordy. I know she met somebody who bowled her over. She told Gail all about it." Star sighed and shifted in bed. "It's…never mind.," she trailed off.

He uttered a chain of words in a language that she couldn't understand. She needed no translation to know that he was swearing.

Swinging his legs over the edge of the bed, he stood up, "I'm going downstairs to have a hot drink. If you want to join me, there's a robe in the closet." He sounded different somehow, closed and pained.

She didn't want to hurt him. He'd shown her the utmost respect and consideration. What was wrong with her, anyway?

CHAPTER 9

Left alone in Daran's bed, Star laid there for a long time thinking about herself, thinking about Lance and about why he'd been able to inflict such a wound onto her psyche. It had everything to do with her opinion of herself—inflated, that's what it was.

She'd always been the sensible, levelheaded child; Gail was the flighty one. Although she was three years younger than her sister, Star recalled hearing references to her greater maturity from their numerous relatives. Star was the responsible one, the one with the settled mind, and the one who more often than not was put in charge of a task. "She's a little woman already," the women in the family often remarked, "whereas that Gail won't ever need wings to fly; she's already up in the air."

Not mean or spiteful by nature, Star never lorded this lofty status over her sister. Gail wouldn't have cared anyway. Being highly creative, as her teachers described her, Gail had so many projects going— writing plays, writing song lyrics, writing letters to her pen pals in French, designing and sewing clothes— that her chores were annoying to her. "Just think," she'd say to Star, "if we didn't have to pick all these apples and peaches for Grandma to can, I could have finished making that outfit for that fallen woman in my play."

When they became teenagers, everyone in the family was terrified that Gail would get pregnant before she graduated from high school. Star and everyone else in the family and all the family friends were informally organized into a "Gail Watch."

Gail couldn't understand how she generated this level of frenzied worry. "I'm never going to let any man mess me over; I've seen too much of that going on around here," she told Star once when Star had broached the subject with her.

No one, on the other hand, felt that Star needed watching. When boys began calling the house to talk to Star, Uncle Nate and Aunt Mellie would exchange smiles and make remarks about "puppy love."

Finally Gail graduated from high school and was offered a scholarship to Hampton University and a local college. Aunt Mellie insisted that Gail take the one from the local college so that she could be closer to home, especially since Uncle Nate had passed away and Aunt Mellie claimed she needed both the girls nearby.

Gail had complied, but two years later, she dropped out to take a job in Alaska. The family members were convinced that this was the beginning of Gail's downfall. Only Gail would want to live in a cold place like Alaska, they said. But as usual, Gail landed on her feet and wrote a year later saying she was back in school at a San Francisco college.

Meanwhile Star had entered the same local college that Gail had attended. During her third year there, she met Lance at a party. He was a part-time student.

They saw each other sporadically at first, but by the end of the year, they were seeing only each other. She hadn't given in to his intense pressure to sleep with him until her natural curiosity took over. One day she decided, "Why not?" She certainly knew enough to avoid getting pregnant.

As Lance lay snoring next to her after the first time, she had wondered, "Is this all there is?" He pointed out to her that it would get better for her over time. Star began spending weekends at his small apartment over a dry cleaner's. Initially they went out a lot. After a while, though, as soon as she would arrive he would want to have sex, and afterwards he wouldn't feel like going anywhere. If it had been enjoyable to her, she wouldn't have minded as much, but Lance was always impatient and would become irritated when she would ask him to slow down or when she'd try to engage him in foreplay.

"I can't wait," he'd exclaim in a frenzy as he pushed himself into her. Moments later he'd be snoring. Or he'd complain that it took her too long to get ready. "What's wrong with you?" became his defense when she'd tell him that he was selfish.

Just before Star's graduation, Gail came to visit her for a week and met Lance for the first time. Gail spotted his flaws instantly and pointed them out to Star. They argued. It was one of the few times they had ever seriously argued. The funny thing was that she had actually agreed with Gail, but by then Lance had become a habit. Star had too much invested in their relationship to easily discard him.

In later arguments with Lance, she found herself repeating Gail's opinions of him, opinions so like her own. She began staying away from his apartment on weekends. He would come by her place and things would be okay until the next row. And then finally the last row came, and three weeks later the rumors started, the rumors about his marrying that other girl—rumors that turned out to be true.

Now, as Star rose from Daran's bed, she squeezed her eyes shut, fighting back the painful memories with steely resolve. She found Daran's robe and pushed her arms into its thick cotton sleeves. She huddled into its soft folds and tied the belt. She moved slowly, tentatively toward the staircase, stopping at the large porthole window to catch a glimpse of the stormy waters. Nothing was visible, but she could hear waves crashing against the shore.

Glancing over the railing and down into the living room, she could neither see nor hear Daran. Maybe he's fallen asleep, she thought. Star padded down the hardwood stairs. She'd almost reached the bottom when she saw him standing in the dining nook gazing out of a porthole window identical to the one she'd left just seconds before. She made a small noise.

He turned around and smiled. His eyes swept her face. "Were you afraid, Starmaine?" Not waiting for a response, he continued, "Don't be. This house is as hurricane-proof as possible. Trust me. It's securely anchored. I had additional pilings installed below sea level just to make sure. I am a civil engineer, you know. I certainly don't plan to be carried away by any storm."

Her eyes took in the high ceilings and open spaces of the large living room, dining nook, and kitchen area. The black, white, beige, and warm brown neutral tones of the walls, wooden floor, and kitchen cabinetry created a striking effect heightened by the few aesthetically harmonious accent pieces. A thick wine and beige plaid rug covered the expanse of wood floor in front of a long black sofa. Marveling at the man's taste, character, and accomplishments, she inquired, "Is there anything you can't do?"

The question seemed to throw him momentarily. "Oh, you mean this." He gestured to their plush surroundings.

"Not only this, your house and property up in Blueberry Run and...you're obviously very successful."

His eyes scoured her face before he spoke. "I can't make you feel me, Starmaine. I can't make you relax with me, at least not for long. I can't make you trust me. That starts the list of things that I can't do, and that's what's most important to me now," he said softly.

A sob welled up inside of her, but she managed to squelch it, but when she began speaking there was still a big lump lodged in her throat. "I was betrayed and humiliated by a man once. It was my first experience, and even though I knew the relationship wouldn't work, I never expected him to do what he did. I spent a lot of time with him, and yet if he had been a murderer, he could have killed me and I wouldn't have had any inkling what he was capable of doing." She blinked quickly to check her tears. "I trusted him completely. It just never occurred to me not to trust him, just like it never occurred to me that he would just marry another woman without telling me first. Up until the day he married her, I was thinking that we still had a relationship, even if it was a bad one. Some judgment I have."

"Well, that's a terrible shame," he said in a thickly sarcastic tone. "You mean you couldn't even predict the future? You couldn't even tell that the guy was a rat before he broke your heart!" His tone mellowed to forestall the angry words that he saw welling up in her. "Where'd you ever get the notion that you're perfect, Starmaine? That you can't make mistakes? You made the same mistake millions of others make every single day as they try to find a life mate." He spread his fingers expansively in an appeal to her logic.

"Don't try to make me feel better by telling me it was not my fault!" she spat. "If I don't know how to steer clear of the Lances of the world, then how is anyone going to do it for me? Who's going to keep me from getting involved with another Lance?" Her eyes blazed at him. "You might even be a Lance type!" As soon as she shot this at him, she felt miserable for saying it. Gail was right. Lance was poisoning her feelings toward any man that became close to her.

"Daran, I'm sorry I said that, but you don't know what—"

"Oh no, Starmaine, don't tell me I don't know what it's like," he said, warding off her apology and explanation. "My ex-wife made deception and adultery into a fine art. She did this for three years before I found out, so I know what it's like to find out that you've been living a lie. It hurt. And it was humiliating. But once I thought about it, I realized that nothing I could have done would have made the ending any different. She was missing something that I could never give her because the void was too deep. With each of those men, she thought she could fill that void. She never did. Now she's in counseling."

His voice softened as he continued. "You couldn't make the guy over, Starmaine. The guy was a rat. That was his makeup, for whatever reason. And rats don't go around wearing a sign announcing what they are. What were you supposed to do, cast a spell on him to make him show his true colors?" He stopped and squinted at her, feigning a look of terror. "You're not a witch, are you?"

She pursed her lips and threw him a malevolent glare. He laughed then, and she realized she'd never heard him really laugh before. The laugh took charge of his whole body and he sank to one knee near the sofa and held on to its arm for support as his body shook.

His laughter was infectious. She felt herself smiling. Then she began to chuckle, and soon she was laughing too. The laugh had a cathartic effect on her and somehow made him even more attractive. She moved toward him and took the hand he held out to her. There was an abundance of both relief and joy in that laugh. If you could laugh at something, it couldn't be that bad or serious. Somehow laughing at a thing put it into perspective.

"This world is crazy," he said, finally getting his breath back. He got to his feet and then sat down on the voluminous sofa, pulling her down next to him. Burying his face in her neck, he nuzzled and moaned. "Mmmmm, you smell so good and you're so soft."

Again, he had ignited a fire within her that instantly blazed out of control. When his hand moved down to slide inside her robe, she was the one who pulled the robe open, hungry to feel his strong and expert fingers on her flesh. He sought her mouth with his own as her mouth opened in anticipation. His tongue slid inside, meeting hers and dueling with it. He planted small kisses around her mouth and nibbled at her full bottom lip for long moments as he rolled her nipples between his fingers. Soon she began to moan ardently. That familiar intensity was building rapidly inside her, screaming for release.

Instinctively, she reached to touch him and her eyes shot open when she touched his sex. It was thick and throbbing. The towel that he'd wrapped around him could not contain it. She sucked her breath in sharply. "Daran," she moaned.

He groaned and his body trembled so hard that she knew he couldn't take much more. He raised his mouth from hers and, staring into her eyes, said in a guttural voice, "Look at it, my darling."

She slowly took her eyes from his eyes, which were clouded with desire. She looked at his manhood. It stood out from his body, big and bold, seemingly waiting for her orders. Her tongue ran over her dry lips, causing them to glisten. She had never known such desire. She'd never even suspected that looking at a man could cause such wild abandon to churn inside her.

His gaze fastened on her lips. "I want to make love to you so badly, Starmaine, that I ache." His hand suddenly slid between her legs and he began to stroke her center. At first she clamped his hand there with her thighs.

"Don't worry, it's not going anywhere," he said gently, pushing her down on the sofa and murmuring against her skin as he rained soft kisses on her cheeks and mouth. "From the first, I had so many thoughts and dreams about our being together like this, thoughts a man should never have about another man's woman, many different dreams like the one I told you, dreams that caused me to wake up hard, lonely, and jealous as hell that he could touch you like this. You've cheated us out of time, Starmaine. But no more. Tonight belongs to me, to us. Let me give you pleasure, Starmaine," he said. "Just do what I say. Just relax and do what I say."

She was virtually delirious by now. Everything about this man gave her pleasure. His voice, which could range from a soft whisper to a growl. His touch, which gave her mind-bending pleasure. His berry-brown eyes, which clouded over with the desire she evoked. The sight of his dark and smooth muscular body.

Star lay back on the couch and gave herself up to his bidding. She felt his fingers open the robe that was somehow still belted. He drew the robe apart and devoured her mounds and valleys with his eyes for a long moment. He breathed heavily. His eyes roamed the length of her, seemingly unable to get enough of her. His fingers began to stroke her center again, and with each caress, her mind and body spun a little closer to the edge of the abyss. The fever that he'd started in her weeks ago had turned into a fully raging fire and she writhed and moaned now for relief from this torture.

Tears slid from her eyes as her buttocks instinctively made frenzied, swirling movements around and upwards in an age-old pattern.

"Daran, please! Daran, Daran," Star moaned as her whole body squirmed to be touched. Uncontrollably the tears rolled back into her hair. This man was arousing unbearable ecstasy in her.

"Starmaine, stop! Damn it! I won't be able to control myself if you keep that up. I want to slide into you right now," he said, his voice ragged. His lips then captured her left nipple and his tongue tortured it with the slightest flicking.

"Mmmmmmmm.!" he murmured. "You're so wet and ready, I can just imagine how it would feel. To slide into you and move inside you, to feel you moving under me as I squeeze your beautiful behind while hearing you moan in my ear."

Suddenly he separated her thighs and she felt his fingers gently part the lips of her feminine center. His eyes ravaged her. Then he began to ever so gently stroke her there again. She flung one leg up over the back of the sofa and gave herself up to the pleasure of his deft fingers. She wanted more, and dug her fingers into his shoulder as she struggled to pull his trembling body onto hers, to complete the union that she desired. But he did not budge from where he kneeled next to the sofa.

The touch of his fingers stroking that tender spot hurled her further toward a vortex of bliss. A moment later, she arched her back and snapped her thighs shut on his thrusting finger sliding into her.

"Daran!" she screamed as her eyes flew open and wave after wave of relief flowed from her. With one hand, she gripped the sofa; with the other, she clutched his shoulder, anchoring herself as she went spinning into a chasm whose walls were velvety soft, where she bounced once and then floated like a butterfly.

She heard his voice, distorted by his own desire, as he commanded, "Open your lovely thighs,

Starmaine. I want to see the moisture glisten between them. Give me the pleasure of looking. I can't do anything else."

His body became noticeably rigid as she parted her thighs. Through the slits of her eyelids, she saw him inhale deeply several times. His voice was hoarse and whispery as he spoke. "Damn it! The way you smell excites me so much! Do you know that, Starmaine? From the first day, every time I think about you, I remember your scent and I get aroused."

He lifted her and carried her up the stairs. Starmaine's head bobbed lazily as he mounted the stairs. Somewhere in the recesses of her mind, she told herself, "You ought to be ashamed of yourself, letting this man carry you around as naked as a peeled grape, letting him touch you and handle you like a piece of meat." Then her other little voice squealed: "But, honey, he sure knows what he's doing." Star smiled.

She was still smiling as he placed her on the bed. Fumbling in the dark, he turned on a lamp that threw a dim beam of light in a corner that filtered throughout the room. Raising herself on one elbow, she tried to sit up.

"Daran, I…" She stopped, awed by the sight of the sheer masculinity of his dark-brown, firmly muscled body. Star was also struck by the confidence and control he exuded. In the bedroom, just as anywhere else, he was in control. Yet despite connections, money, and power, he was extremely solicitous of her feelings and caring of her welfare, even now when many men would have selfishly sated their lust.

Marveling at the control he displayed under the circumstances, she openly looked at his arousal. It stuck out, turgid—seemingly commanding her attention.

Star's breaths quickened. She clenched her lower lip between her teeth as she felt a quickening at the base of her abdomen. Her eyes traveled slowly up his torso to his face. She blushed. He had been looking at her look at him. She averted her eyes.

"No, don't look away, my darling. You want me. You want it. And this"—he looked down at his erection—"will be a permanent condition for me until you do something about it."

Her eyes followed his to where he was rigid and thick. "It excites me for you to look at me like that," he whispered. Staring into her eyes, he slowly crawled toward her on the king-size bed. "Everything about you excites me," he growled as he propped himself up on one elbow over her. Lowering his face to hers, he used the tip of his tongue to draw circles around her lips. The hot moistness of his tongue set off wanton sensations in Star. Her lips captured his tongue and drew on it. He moaned and his fingers began to knead her abdomen softly, moving ever lower to the triangle beneath. His fingers did not linger there this time. Instead, he caressed the satiny softness inside her full thighs.

Star reached then for his throbbing male hardness. She felt him swell even larger in her hand. She wrapped her fingers around him snugly and slid her hand up and down its shaft. Her fingers seemed to have a mind of their own, sliding the length of him from base to tip. She was amazed at her boldness, but his responding body movements and sounds of joy told her that she was giving him the most infinite pleasure a woman can ignite in a man.

His tongue thrust deeply into her mouth as his passion took over. He emitted low groans, sounds so guttural that Star thought he had reached the point of no return.

Then his mouth was nuzzling her neck as he implored her, "Open your thighs, my darling, and lie still. Whatever you do, don't move." With his knees, he nudged her legs apart. His breathing was ragged. His mouth had moved to her breast, where it slowly pulled on her taut nipple.

Fearing that his admirable self-control had finally worn away, Star wrenched away from him in the huge bed. She summoned up the dregs of her own self-control and with as much conviction as she could unconvincingly murmured, "Daran, let's stop this now. As you said, we don't want to do anything we'll regret."

"I won't ever regret this," he said. Cupping her buttocks in his hands, he lifted the lower part of her body off the bed and smothered his face in her. He began to murmur lascivious endearments about her smell, her taste, and her anatomy while his lips and tongue launched an assault on her that caused the blood to drum ferociously in her ears. She was aroused to an inconceivable level of passion. How could her mouth say no when her body screamed yes?

Then suddenly and unpredictably, he lowered her back to the bed. She pressed her thighs together even though his hands were still beneath her.

"Relax. Just open your thighs and relax. You've got to learn to feel freedom with me," he coaxed, withdrawing his hands. "I'm not going to pounce on you. I could have done that an hour ago. Just give yourself up to the beauty of this night. Give yourself to me, Starmaine. That's what I want. I want you to feel me. I want to be a part of your spirit, your consciousness, as well as your flesh. Starmaine, I cherish you."

Star moaned. A sob tore through her throat as she lay in this man's bed, in his arms, in his power. And she had never felt safer or more secure. She relaxed then and did his bidding.

As soon as she spread her legs, he pressed his turgid, velvety shaft against the inner folds of her feminine cradle, being careful that in his urgency, he did not hurt her.

"Ah, Starmaine. I'm in heaven now. And whatever you do, don't move," he growled into her ear. He held her so very tightly that moving was out of the question. She knew he was fighting for the control he needed to prevent plunging into her.

He began to move then, slowly, tremulously sliding his shaft against the tender flesh of her slippery triangle. Wave after wave of thunderous pleasure overwhelmed her, rendering her mindless.

His climax was immediate and convulsive, and he held her tightly crushed against him as words of joy spilled from his mouth.

She sobbed then, hot, salty tears.

He was instantly solicitous. "Did I hurt you? You felt so good." Then he touched her intimately. "It felt so good that I just lost…" His whole body jerked as if to show the feeling that words could not fully convey.

No, he hadn't hurt her, she assured him as she continued to sob. Strangely, though he soothed her, he did not try to make her stop crying. In that extremely perceptive way of his, he seemed to understand that she needed to cry—to rid herself of the humiliation, pain, and anger from her past. Maybe he understood because he too had been hurt. Pain understood pain.

Daran pulled her close and wiped her tears away with his fingers. At that moment, her tears changed to tears of joy-joy for having found or been found by a man like Daran. She fell asleep in his arms. All through the night, his hands and mouth moved over her body. She was awakened several times by him as he worked her body into an orgasmic fervor, as his fingers and mouth prodded, stroked, nibbled, caressed, and probed every inch of her body. Star climaxed explosively each time. And throughout the night, she felt his male hardness throbbing feverishly as he kept it pressed against her, as if it belonged to her.

CHAPTER 10

Starmaine pinched her eyelids shut as ribbons of sunlight intruded on a dream set somewhere in an exotic, tropical environment. For some strange reason, her heart was racing as if unsuspected danger lurked in the lush tropical flora. Sleep was fast receding as she struggled to hang on to the dream long enough to find out what the plants would reveal.

Becoming fully awake suddenly, she opened her eyes as the last snatches of the dream disappeared from her conscious mind.

As she flung her arm against the pillow beside her, her hand brushed against a sheet of notepaper that lay atop the pillow. She frowned, seeing that the bed was empty except for her, then concluded that Daran must have gone out to inspect for storm damage.

Noticing the piece of paper again, she picked it up. "We must always be together. Will you marry me?" leapt from the paper.

Starmaine's heart romped wildly and a spasm of liquid heat flitted through her as she read the words again. Recalling the night before, she became flushed.

"Daran?" she called out. Silence greeted her.

"He wouldn't leave a written marriage proposal if he were here, silly," she scolded herself, lightheaded with happiness.

Wrapping a sheet around her body, still tender from their lovemaking, she padded toward the bathroom but stopped midway as the details of the dream and their significance shot through her mind.

I can't marry him! I can never marry him! These words were cold and flat. They tasted bitter as she mouthed them again and again.

What had he said that night at Tiger's restaurant? "I'm an African and I'll always be an African. One day I'll go home to stay. The urge is always there."

The dream! It had been a way of warning her to avoid tropical settings by avoiding men from those settings.

Star shut her eyes tight as she tried to see if she could press him out of her mind. She shivered as the stark memory of Daran's full effect loomed large and in living color. "I'm in heaven, now," he kept whispering. She could imagine him standing before her, his rich dark skin and lean muscles causing her mind-bending excitement.

And Star had to admit that she too had been in heaven in his arms or whenever he was around her. He'd had that effect on her from the beginning.

A tear rolled down her face as she realized that she loved him. If she were to marry him, no amount of heavenly love would make him want to stay away from his home in Nigeria, not permanently. She knew that one day, as he'd said, that urge would compel him to go home to stay. It could be next year or five years from now, but one day he would. She would never ask him to give up his home to stay in the United States, with her and the children.

And she couldn't give up her home, her family, and all the things that were dear and familiar to her, to live permanently on the other side of the world. She loved him, but either way, one of them would end up unhappy. That had to be faced squarely before it was too late.

The ringing of the phone pulled her from her reverie. She knew it was him. Who else would it be? She lifted the receiver. "Hello," she croaked. Her throat suddenly had a lump in it.

"Hi, sweetie. Did I wake you?" His voice was vibrant.

"No, I've been awake for a while."

"Your voice is exciting me," he whispered.

Star gripped the receiver. What she said now would ultimately save them both from a lot of misery.

"Daran, did you check on the car?"

Deafening silence yawned through the line for long moments.

"Did you read the note I left?"

"I read it."

"Well?"

She knew she had to be strong and firm. Her armor had to be impenetrable or else he would find a way to weaken and ultimately defeat her on this. She would take refuge in nonchalance.

"Just because we spent a night in bed together does not mean you have to marry me, Daran. Chivalry is dead, remember? Besides, we didn't even go all the way."

"Damn you, Starmaine!"

She was perspiring. She never realized how much energy it took to be nonchalant. But she had to make her point, so she plowed on. "Listen carefully, Daran. It was a lovely, tender night between a man and a woman. I will treasure it always. I especially appreciate how you restrained yourself . But now in the light of day, we can see that it was just one night and have no regrets."

"That's a pretty speech, Starmaine. Bravo!" His voice shot angry sparks at her. "I'm bringing the car. I'll be there in a few minutes."

"I won't be here." Star realized that he had found a chink in her armor and was forcing her to retreat— at least a few steps.

"You don't have a choice—you don't have a car, remember?"

"I'll call a cab," she threatened.

Silence again.

"Oh, so that's the way it's to be." He laughed.

"Okay, Starmaine. I can play this game, too. You should have just said you needed time to think about our marriage."

"No, Daran," she said through clenched teeth. "I don't need time to think. I'm not going to marry you—ever. Just drop off the damn car and stop acting like you're some kind of swami who knows me better than I know myself."

He laughed again. "Wrong culture. I would be a witch doctor, not a swami." "Same difference. You know what I mean!" Her voice rose. "Okay, okay, I'll drop the car off and I won't press you now. Good-bye, my darling. I'll see you later."

The receiver hummed in her hand and Starmaine looked at it a long time before she placed it in its cradle and headed toward the shower.

She arrived at the Placido just before one o'clock. Rex, she learned, would be absent due to an illness in the family. She made a mental note to call to inquire about his daughter's health and to tell him he could pick up his car at the Placido's garage.

After picking up her messages, she went into her office and closed the door. She wanted to be alone to think about the night before. Trouble was, the more she thought about it, about Daran, the more confused and disturbed she became.

Using all her willpower to shove the incident from her mind, she called Gail to let her know what had happened to wreck her plans with Rex. She schooled herself not to hint at or mention anything else.

"Guess who stopped by a few minutes ago to leave a package for you?" Gail asked cheerfully.

"Who?" Star was puzzled. She sometimes received packages and books related to her work, but they were always delivered to the spa.

"Daran."

"What kind of package?" Had he taken some sort of memento from their night together and was returning it to embarrass her?

"Well, actually, he had me open it to get my opinion on whether you'd like it."

Suddenly nervous, Star did a quick inventory of her clothing and few jewelry items. Everything was accounted for. What could he have of hers? This is crazy, she thought. He wouldn't take some article of mine and ask Gail's opinion.

"Are you there, Star?" Gail's voice had that triumphant tone that told Star she was enjoying every minute of the suspense.

"Yeah. I was just wondering why the guy would be dropping off a package for me."

"He said it was an engagement gift," Gail said, chuckling.

"Engagement? You're kidding! I certainly have no intentions of marrying him."

"But he did propose?"

"Obviously. You mean you don't know all the details?" Star said, wondering if he'd told Gail about their night together.

"Now, Star, before you get mad. He explained to me that marriage in his culture is a union of two families, not just two individuals. He said that in Nigeria, his family would have visited our family and the marriage would be discussed like a joint venture."

"How romantic! Would they sell shares in this corporate marriage?"

"Star. Stop that! I'm just trying to remember some of the things he said. He said that the marriage becomes both families' affair. You would be marrying into his family—you'd be his family's wife, girl!"

"It's like, marry one and get the rest for free!"

"It's something you two have to talk about. It's another culture, after all."

"That's the point, Gail! Two different cultures…" The futility of the situation, of the discussion, rose up suddenly before Star and made her tired. "Gail, I've got to go. I'll see you tomorrow. All that driving has made me too tired to make the drive down there tonight. Besides, Larry's coming home tonight, isn't he?"

"Yes, some time this afternoon. I'm not even going to let Nanny sleep today. She can do all her sleeping tonight so that we'll have the whole house to ourselves. And you know I'm not going to work tomorrow. I've already called in sick. And Larry had better not be tired either 'cause I have been deprived for too long!"

"You'd better go and get all dolled up for Larry and I'd better get to work. See you Tuesday, sister dear," Star said, breaking the connection. She could gab with her sister all afternoon and never get any work done. A few moments later, she realized that she hadn't asked her sister what the package contained. Although she was curious, she knew whatever it was would only complicate the matter more.

For the next two hours, Star struggled to concentrate on paperwork. But all too often she had to yank her mind back from thoughts of Daran.

Forget him, she ordered herself. She could and she would forget the slight gap between his two front teeth, the way his white teeth contrasted so starkly with his black-brown skin, the jolting effect of the purple tinge in his brown eyes that made them look wine-colored when the light struck them or when he was in the throes of passion, the deftness of his fingers as they probed and stroked, his mouth on her breasts, her cries and his whispers of heavenly bliss, the tremors that rocked his body and her soul!

She could forget, couldn't she? Star squeezed her eyes shut and then clenched her fists so tight her fingernails came dangerously close to drawing blood.

At five P.M., she announced that she was going home. "Not feeling well," she explained to Deidra, dashing for the elevator. Its doors slid closed, blocking Star's view of the receptionist's puzzled face. Star knew that she was being uncharacteristically melancholy and curt, but all she could think about right now was getting to the condo, taking a shower, and jumping into bed.

By six-thirty, she'd accomplished the first two. She'd just dried off and slid into a sleeveless tunic-length nightie when the doorbell rang.

Her first thought was to ignore it, but when it kept ringing, she worried it might be something important. She grabbed a robe and ran down the stairs. "Coming!" she called out. The doorbell rang again just as she reached the door. Annoyed, she muttered, "Any knucklehead should assume that it takes a few seconds to get to the door."

As she peered through the peephole, her annoyance was replaced by fear mingled with surprise. It was Daran!

She opened the door as his hand rose to ring the bell again. He smiled. "Hello, Starmaine," he said, and strolled through the door before Star could react. He pushed the door shut behind him and turned the deadbolt lock. Turning toward her, his eyes slid from her ankles up her long, bare legs and thighs and on up to where her breasts strained at the cotton knit fabric of the tunic.

His eyes clouded over with turbulent emotion and watching the storm rage in them, Star shivered as her legs suddenly became rubbery.

"Put your robe on, Starmaine," he said huskily, nodding at the robe she clutched in her hand. "We have to talk."

"H-How'd you know I was here?" She struggled to regain her composure as electrical currents lashed through her.

"I called the Placido and they said you'd gone home. I figured you'd come here since you'd want to give Larry and Gail some time together—alone." He gave her a knowing look and chuckled. "And of course I knew where this place was because I followed you here a few weeks ago." He paused as he saw her brow wrinkle. "Remember? From the restaurant."

"Followed me?" she mouthed. "Followed me?" she repeated as she remembered back to that night at the Windjammer. She could have sworn that he and his client left before she and Rex did.

"I'm sorry if that disturbs you, but I'm not sorry I did it." He sauntered around the room, examining objects—books, paperweights, fingering the leaves of the large foliage plants as he talked. "Even then, I knew you were the woman for me, Starmaine. I was strongly attracted to you from that first day when you opened the door in your pink leotard. As a matter of fact, I was momentarily insane. You'll never know how close I came to going against my cultural background and my own personal code of morality."

He turned to face her now as he said, "I wanted to make hot, swift love to you, right there in the foyer of Larry's house. Later, I laughed at myself and chalked it up to being horny. I haven't been with a woman for over a year now, Starmaine."

He swallowed and looked at her intently, forcing her to understand his meaning. "At least not the way a man wants to be with a woman," he added softly. Turning abruptly from her, he stepped onto the stairway leading up to the main floor that housed the condo's spacious living room and kitchen.

"What's up here?" he called over his shoulder as he climbed the stairs.

Starmaine was flooded by a multitude of conflicting emotions: she wanted him there, but she didn't; she did not want him to touch her, but she did; she wanted to marry him, but she wouldn't, she couldn't.

Though, when he was around her, things certainly just seemed to crackle and pop. She couldn't help smiling at herself for comparing him to a cereal. She still smiled as she followed him up the stairs.

Daran's eyes took in the tasteful decor of the large, cathedral-ceilinged room in a glance. Her favorite colors were pinks and purples—they made a gorgeous backdrop for her honey-toned skin. The lavender robe, belted snugly now, and the short nightie she wore underneath proved to him beyond any doubt that she was extremely delectable in those colors. Or was he instead looking at the way the soft fabric clung to her curves?

Her full breasts beckoned him urgently, but he would ignore their call, at least for now. It wasn't the colors or the clothes she wore that drove him to distraction. It was what was underneath those clothes, as well as her smell and the soft, satiny texture of her skin, her smile, the short, asymmetrical cut of her hair, the way she completed him. He wanted her with such intensity it would be unbearable if she proved to be unattainable.

"I talked to Gail before I came here," he said, looking out through the patio doors at the view of the valley.

"That figures," she said, slapping her hands against her thighs. "You and my sister certainly seem to have a lot to talk about!"

"Jealous?" he inquired, turning toward her as that easy smile slid over his features.

"Don't try to change the subject!" she snapped. Star's annoyance with the whole situation was mounting. They might as well just have it out. Then she could go on with her life as it had been before. "Every time I don't play it your way, you go to my sister and get her to try to soften me up. That irks me, Daran! After I told you I wasn't Larry's wife, you wanted me to go out with you. But instead of just asking me out and accepting whatever my answer might have been, you drop in to see Gail.

"Next thing I know, you're invited over for a drink and chitchat. That way you got to be with me even though I wouldn't go out with you. And you kept on doing that—working your way into my sister's good graces so that you can get her to influence me." Star was almost breathless what with all the angry energy that was surging through her.

Throughout it all, Daran stood and watched every movement and facial expression of this spirited woman. Her usually soft eyes flashed, and in her anger she had the cutest way of shutting her eyes while opening her mouth.

He had never seen her so angry or so desirable. And damned if he wasn't getting aroused!

He used his own anger to mask his arousal. "Well, how in the world was I supposed to get you to be with me? You're so standoffish and defensive. It wasn't me who first said, 'All's fair in love and war,' right? That's what I told myself the night I moved your cart—I wanted to get a reaction from you, to see what you were like. I certainly got my curiosity satisfied. You saw the way I watched my back, right?" He chuckled and Star felt her anger begin to melt. This man could always muffle her thunder by making her want to smile or laugh.

"I knew from that incident that you had a lot of spirit, even though you have a smooth, businesslike exterior. I knew that you were my kind of woman, Starmaine—spirited, determined, very attractive." Then almost inaudibly he added, "And very passionate." He moved a step toward her, but she backed away. He continued, "I knew we'd meet again; after all, Blueberry Run is a small town. Under what circumstances I didn't know, but I knew it would happen. And I knew I wanted you. I want you, Starmaine."

"The point here is that if I were to marry you, Daran, the marriage would not survive. Getting married is easy. The hard part is staying married. You would want to go back to Africa one day, to live there permanently, and I would not want to stay there for the rest of my life. And what if there are children? I want children one day and I want them to have a regular life." Star stopped. All this talk about marriage, the future and children suddenly made her sad; although Daran would be a wonderful husband and father and they could have a wonderful life together, it was simply not to be.

"There you go again, Starmaine, trying to predict the future. Remember, you didn't do so well the first time."

"How dare you bring that up now? How dare you use that against—"

"I'm not using it against you! I'm using it to help you to see that nothing is carved in stone. Lots of perfectly matched couples end up with perfectly failed marriages. Then there are lots of people who have lots of differences, and they make their marriages work. You know why their marriages work? It's because they decide they're going to work, no matter what. They make them work. I believe in making things happen, making them work. That's all you have to decide. That's all you have to do. I've already committed myself to that, to making us work. And besides, what's so different about us?" He smiled. "You're an African woman even if you don't know how to pound yams and make fufu!"

"That's just it, Daran," she persisted, refusing to be put off by his light-hearted humor this time. "I'm not an African woman. I'm an African American woman who has lived all her life in the USA. This is my culture, not because I chose it; I just happened to have been born and bred here. I've read a lot and I've heard a lot about so many things that go wrong in these types of marriages. You might be one way with me here, but when we go to Africa, you might change on me. And I won't tolerate that."

"Oh, you mean I will marry nine other women so that I'll have ten wives—a nice round number, of course. But just think: because I'm considered one of those rich Africans, I'll have to buy each of you a white Mercedes to match my white limo. And of course you'll all wear so much gold jewelry that you won't be able to walk and you'll have to be carried on gold chairs by miserable, downtrodden natives. And naturally you'll each have ten children, all boys, of course, because everyone knows that African men hate female children. And if you can't have children, I'll have the local witch doctor poison you and my faithful, native servants will bury you in the deepest, darkest jungle of Africa. Or…"

He dropped to one knee and held up his hands in the melodramatic pose of a mad director. "Wait, I'm getting another scenario. How about one day you find out how I've managed to hide my tail? You will of course tell your story to the *National Enquirer:* 'How Africans Hide Their Tails' as told by an African American woman who was married to one of the beasts! You'll become an instant celebrity because you will have vindicated all those who have been trying for centuries to prove to the world that Africans are not fully human." He stopped and looked at her.

She sighed.

"Those are just some of the images of Africa and Africans that keep Africans and blacks outside of Africa apart, Starmaine."

"Yes, Daran."

"Yes?" He eyed her, wondering if she had even been listening.

"Yes, I will marry you."

His mouth fell open. He stared at her, then shook his head. She had never seen him look like this before.

"I hope you didn't have this change of heart because you want to prove to me that you are not misguided about Africans."

"That's ridiculous," she said as she took a step toward him. "I just suddenly realized that I believe in you, and more importantly; in us." She didn't get a chance to take another step because in one movement he pulled her against him, crushing her against his muscular body. Through the soft fabric of her nightie and robe, Starmaine could feel his impassioned desire, throbbing expectantly. His hands slid down to her buttocks and cupped them as she moved her body against his. The familiar ache in her loins settled at the top of her thighs. She arched her body against his.

"You've made me so happy," he said as he kissed her brow, her nose, and her eyelids, and trailed little kisses to her mouth, slowly at first, then hungrily as they explored each other's mouths intimately and urgently. As her hands slid beneath his polo shirt, touching the bare flesh of his smooth back, a rumbling moan started deep inside him.

"The bed," he muttered against her mouth. He tore his mouth from hers and added, "I want to love you in bed, Starmaine." He did not wait for a response but planted a trail of feverish kisses down her throat, at the hollow of her neck, and on her breasts, where his lips nipped at one hardened nipple through the thin fabric of her nightie.

With his head, he nudged the spaghetti straps of her nightie off her shoulders. She shook the remnants of the robe off her body and it slid to the floor. The nightie followed in its path but was caught by the curve of her hips, her bare breasts exposed.

Overwhelmed by her beauty, he stepped back and stared.

She stood there, arms at her side, excited beyond reason. She shivered before the torment in his berry-brown eyes.

"Heavenly," he murmured over and over as his eyes moved from one honey-colored nipple to the other. Surrounded by their darkened aureoles, her sensitive nipples hardened as he looked at them. Transfixed by their loveliness, he reached out and with gentle, painstaking slowness drew his palm across them.

Starmaine gasped as pleasure rippled through her. Her knees quaked.

"Daran?" she called in a high, pleading voice that was barely recognizable. He understood the question and the need that her tone held. "Yes, my darling. I'm ready this time."

She turned and moved on rubbery legs toward another flight of stairs that led up to another floor. He followed her, shedding his clothes. By the time they reached the room that contained her queen-size bed, he wore only his briefs and she nothing at all. His manhood bulged threateningly against the cotton knit fabric of his shorts, but he waited for her to turn around before he slid them off slowly.

"Do you see what you've done to me?" he asked softly as his eyes traveled slowly from her face to her honey-colored nipples. He slid on a condom as she watched. "Talk to me, Starmaine, tell me what you plan to do about my condition."

In answer, she held out her arms to him and they fell back on the bed, crying out their joy at the delectable sensations their bodies gave each other.

Star parted her legs, anxious to have him inside her, but he did not oblige. Instead, his hand began to ever so lightly stroke her center. Her eyes fluttered shut as she threatened to climax.

"No, Starmaine, keep your eyes open. I want to see the pleasure that you're feeling. I want to look into your eyes as I enter you," he said softly.

"Now, Daran! Now, please," she sobbed as desire flooded her body and every nerve screamed for release.

He poised himself above her then, and as her body arched toward him, he entered her with one fluid movement. Her eyes stretched wide, staring into his, reflecting the pleasure he gave her as clearly as mirrors. He felt like he was drowning in the pleasure he saw there. Then, as if the struggle was too great, her lashes came together.

The expression on her face set off a violent tremor in him and he was afraid to move, afraid he would climax and disappoint her; but also afraid that if he couldn't control the wayward fire that rampaged his loins, he would climax anyway so great was his need.

Struggling for the briefest control, he began to move slowly, thrusting as deeply as he dared, fearful that he might hurt her. She was as tight as a sheath at first but she quickly responded, and her moistness made him less fearful that his thrusts would hurt her.

As she began to respond to his every stroke, Star's need knew no bounds and she wrapped her legs around his back.

This simple act inflamed him and propelled him to bury himself deeply into the luscious recesses of her femininity. Daran became lost in the bliss he found there, lost in time and space. And as his body released into hers, it was as if he followed the wake of an exploding star, shattering into pieces that fell silently into the satiny darkness.

Star lay on her back beside him, listening to his breathing. She was reluctant to shift her position for fear she would wake him, but she knew the instant he opened his eyes because she felt them on her.

She turned toward him, and when her eyes met his, an easy smile crept over his features. He looked at her sheepishly.

"Do you always faint when you make love to a woman?" she inquired.

He grinned and pulled her to him possessively. "You felt so good to me that my mind just went around the bend. I just lost myself." He chuckled and touched her feminine triangle. "I hope I didn't hurt you."

Noting the concern in his voice, she covered his hand with her own. "No, my darling, every move was magic for me." She touched him suggestively. "As a matter of fact, I can't wait until we do it again."

"Me too," he said, caressing her scalp with his fingertips and sliding his fingers through her short hair. "My mother sent some gold jewelry for you. I'm breaking tradition by not giving it to you at the right times. I tried, though. I left the first piece, a bracelet, with Gail. That's the piece you get when I propose. A necklace is given when you consent to be my wife. That's in my trunk now. Once again, overdue. You get the last two pieces, the ring and the earrings, on the day you become my wife."

"How'd you know I'd marry you?" "Well, I know how persistent I am. I knew it was just a matter of time."

She reached up to trace his hairline, eyebrows, and cheek with her finger, ending at his mouth. "I love you," she said. "I've never told you that."

"I know."

"You know I haven't told you, or you know I love you." "Both." "How do you know I love you?" "No woman could give herself as completely to a man if she didn't love him."

"Oh."

"When will we be married, Starmaine?"

"I don't know. When do you think?"

"I'll leave that up to you," he said, his voice husky as he rolled atop her and nudged her legs apart. "I've got enough to keep me busy for now," he murmured against her temple as he sank deeply into her. "Make it soon, though," he gasped as he began to move. "I want…to be…in heaven every night…all night long."

EPILOGUE

Starmaine scanned the shiny dials and switches on the control panel, looking for the one that controlled the sauna room's steam output. Checking the controls of the machinery at the spa was one of the responsibilities she had reserved for herself when she opened the spa months before. Doing it herself was a necessity because so far she hadn't been able to find anyone to whom she could entrust the duty. She tried to talk Rex into relocating to Africa or to at least come over for a year to train a staff, and Mrs. Akala had offered him a stupendous salary, but he declined the offer, saying he was not ready for such a move.

Starmaine knew that he still felt wounded by her abandonment of him, as he had termed her marriage to Daran and her move to Nigeria. "You're my…" He had stopped, fumbling for the word he sought. "…other, Star, my love, my closest friend. I'm closer to you than to anyone on this earth, Star. I love you. Don't leave me," he had pleaded when she told him about her decision. "If it's a sexual thing, have your fling with your exotic, foreign man. I can accept that."

Then to Star's amazement, Rex began to cry. Nothing she said comforted him. Finally she rose and left the bewildered man sitting in the restaurant booth, recalling as she left that it was the same place he'd brought her on their first date. She hadn't realized the depth of his feelings for her, but even if she had, it wouldn't have made any difference because Daran fulfilled her, completed her.

When she recounted the episode to Daran, he simply said, "It was plain to me that the guy was crazy about you. Now you know why I kept asking Gail about my competition."

They had a late spring wedding, a small one on the lawn of Gail's home. The reception, organized chiefly by Cordy, was at his house. Star's house, too, now he pointed out.

Cordy had taken her aside that evening to announce that Max had asked her to marry him and she accepted, but their marriage would be as Cordy had put it, "back home in Africa." That's what Max wants. I'm so thankful that you came along when you did, Starmaine. If you hadn't, I would've still been pursuing Daran. Contrary, that's what I am. I always want what's hard to get. Then when I get it, I don't want it. This time I was confronted. Max told me I was spoiled and contrary and that I could no longer afford my behavior. And it dawned on me that he was right."

Starmaine and Daran had gone to Egypt for their honeymoon. He knew the place like the back of his hand. "I've been allover Africa in the course of my work," he'd whispered after blissful hours of love-making, "but now I want to do an extended pleasure tour with you, my darling."

Loving morning, noon, and night; sometimes the look would come into his eyes at the oddest of places and he'd say, "I want you. I can't help it, but I want you now." He'd continue talking to her, murmuring, repeating his need for her, brushing against her as he subtly made her aware of his need for her to the point where she'd get so weak and wobbly that they would have to rush back to their hotel to satiate themselves.

During their month-long honeymoon, they had meandered throughout most of East Africa. Star was amazed by the fact that despite the war-torn ravages of the place and the extreme poverty, the residents possessed a vibrancy and sense of hope sadly missing in many blacks in the United States. When she remarked about this to Daran, he pointed out that the culture could be thanked for supplying constant hope and the unrelenting will to survive and prosper.

Daran had said, "The culture has taken into account that there will be hardships, but the individual must prevail and will survive. The current strife is seen as a difficult but brief experience in the history of this very old culture. Unlike blacks in the United States, we have retained our ancient beliefs and traditions, our history, our languages, and our ties to each other. These East Africans still walk on the land their ancestors walked on, and it is these ancestors who whisper to them and keep them warm and feed them with hope until their last breath. We West Africans are the same."

The experience had jolted Star. It had given her a new perspective. When they returned to Blueberry Run, she told Gail of her decision to accept Mrs. Akala's offer to set up and operate a spa at a luxurious hotel on an island in Lagos, Nigeria.

"Star, you'll be so far away! What if something happened to you? Suppose you get sick?" Gail's expressive eyes darted around the room, her imagination rife with all the things that might happen to her younger sister. In the end, tears sprang from her eyes. "Don't pay me any attention. I'll just miss you. I was counting on you living right here in the neighborhood. You're the only family I have now that Aunt Mellie and Uncle Nate are gone. You know how it is: the cousins down south are family in name only."

"Gail, I'll probably be in this country more than I'm in Africa. And you have heard of airplanes, right? They make the world a very small place, and they go in both directions. Now you'll get your chance to come and stay as long as you want without picking up to move there."

"What about your house here? Are you going to sell it when Cordy leaves?"

"Absolutely not. I told you we'll probably be here almost as much as we are in Africa. In our work we both travel a lot and can mix business with pleasure. Don't worry, we'll be here for extended stays. We'll straddle the globe."

Recalling this conversation brought the reality of her present task sharply into focus. Daran had teased her about not being able to delegate. After an assistant could be found and trained, she wouldn't have to do these sorts of things, she pointed out to him, but for now, there was no one else.

Soon her receptionist and the workers from the hotel on the hill would arrive to attend to the myriad other duties that were required to operate a successful spa. Then she could go back up the hill to the hotel and have her morning swim before the hotel guests began to mill around the outside breakfast bar and pool area. After her swim she'd have breakfast with Daran.

Her pulse quickened at the thought of him as it always did. Just being around Daran stimulated her. Just hearing his voice, just being in his presence made her feel warm and secure. He was an inventive, unhurried, and masterful lover and his lovemaking always left her fully satisfied. She loved him even more than she had before, and the more she learned about him, the more she loved him. She knew he returned her love.

Glancing out through the solarium's glass wall, she noticed two large and colorful tropical lizards sitting atop one of the long balcony walls of the room. Smiling, she recalled how terrified she'd been of these animals when she first arrived in Lagos. Her screams had brought the hotel security to the door of the penthouse suite and had caused such a commotion that an amusing article had appeared the following morning in one of Lagos's largest daily newspapers with the headline TERROR AT THE EDONI HOTEL. "Hotel security had been dispatched to combat the terrorists that had besieged the honeymoon suite of a Mr. and Mrs. Daran Ajero. Mrs.

Ajero, an American, screamed so loudly that all the guests on the top floor of the luxurious hotel awakened, panic-stricken. It turned out that the terrorists were none other than an extended family of our local lizards, who the hysterical Mrs. Ajero described as being monstrously large and terrifying."

The article had gone on to talk about the new spa that was about to open at the hotel and mentioned that Mrs. Starmaine Ajero, a noted fitness program developer and consultant, was the proprietor. Coming as it had right before the spa's opening, the article had been wonderful publicity, and from the day of its opening, many wealthy Nigerians as well as European expatriates and visitors had flocked to it.

"Good morning, madam," Juri, her receptionist, said as Star headed for the front door of the spa. Star jumped, startled. "Oh, good morning, Juri. I did not know you were here."

"Madam, I'm always prompt." She sounded slightly offended.

"Sure you are, Juri. I had my mind elsewhere."

Amusement flickered across the young woman's face. "Madam was perhaps thinking about Mr. Ajero."

Star smiled. She and Juri had worked out an easy relationship during the young woman's month of employment at the spa. If she could only get her to stop calling her madam. She asked Juri repeatedly to just call her by her name, but to no avail. She noticed that the West Africans used the term as a respectful way of addressing a married woman. Interestingly, they gave it the French pronunciation: madahm.

"Juri, you know I always go up to the hotel to have breakfast with him," Star said, barely able to conceal a blush.

"Yes, go ahead and enjoy your meal," Juri replied, also smiling.

Walking through the airy lobby of the beautiful hotel almost made Star weep. The decor's varying earth tones—from bleached wood to white sand— washed over her, filling her as smoothly as the harmony of a symphony. Beauty had always had an arresting effect on her. Always it had made her teary-eyed. She had never imagined that a hotel could be so beautiful, so perfect. Its open-air design coupled with its split levels encased in other split levels accentuated its columns and dramatic curves. Edoni Hotel captured the heady beauty that made all of West Africa seem so vibrant and urgent. Star loved the hotel, the country, the continent.

As she walked toward the elevator that would whisk her up to her love, she knew, with the swiftness and certainty of a truth that hits in the middle of the night, that come what may, this place was her home.

2008 Reprint Mass Market Titles
January

Cautious Heart
Cheris F. Hodges
ISBN-13: 978-1-58571-301-1
ISBN-10: 1-58571-301-5
$6.99

Suddenly You
Crystal Hubbard
ISBN-13: 978-1-58571-302-8
ISBN-10: 1-58571-302-3
$6.99

February

Passion
T. T. Henderson
ISBN-13: 978-1-58571-303-5
ISBN-10: 1-58571-303-1
$6.99

Whispers in the Sand
LaFlorya Gauthier
ISBN-13: 978-1-58571-304-2
ISBN-10: 1-58571-304-x
$6.99

March

Life Is Never As It Seems
J. J. Michael
ISBN-13: 978-1-58571-305-9
ISBN-10: 1-58571-305-8
$6.99

Beyond the Rapture
Beverly Clark
ISBN-13: 978-1-58571-306-6
ISBN-10: 1-58571-306-6
$6.99

April

A Heart's Awakening
Veronica Parker
ISBN-13: 978-1-58571-307-3
ISBN-10: 1-58571-307-4
$6.99

Breeze
Robin Lynette Hampton
ISBN-13: 978-1-58571-308-0
ISBN-10: 1-58571-308-2
$6.99

May

I'll Be Your Shelter
Giselle Carmichael
ISBN-13: 978-1-58571-309-7
ISBN-10: 1-58571-309-0
$6.99

Careless Whispers
Rochelle Alers
ISBN-13: 978-1-58571-310-3
ISBN-10: 1-58571-310-4
$6.99

June

Sin
Crystal Rhodes
ISBN-13: 978-1-58571-311-0
ISBN-10: 1-58571-311-2
$6.99

Dark Storm Rising
Chinelu Moore
ISBN-13: 978-1-58571-312-7
ISBN-10: 1-58571-312-0
$6.99

2008 Reprint Mass Market Titles (continued)

July

Object of His Desire
A.C. Arthur
ISBN-13: 978-1-58571-313-4
ISBN-10: 1-58571-313-9
$6.99

Angel's Paradise
Janice Angelique
ISBN-13: 978-1-58571-314-1
ISBN-10: 1-58571-314-7
$6.99

August

Unbreak My Heart
Dar Tomlinson
ISBN-13: 978-1-58571-315-8
ISBN-10: 1-58571-315-5
$6.99

All I Ask
Barbara Keaton
ISBN-13: 978-1-58571-316-5
ISBN-10: 1-58571-316-3
$6.99

September

Icie
Pamela Leigh Starr
ISBN-13: 978-1-58571-275-5
ISBN-10: 1-58571-275-2
$6.99

At Last
Lisa Riley
ISBN-13: 978-1-58571-276-2
ISBN-10: 1-58571-276-0
$6.99

October

Everlastin' Love
Gay G. Gunn
ISBN-13: 978-1-58571-277-9
ISBN-10: 1-58571-277-9
$6.99

Three Wishes
Seressia Glass
ISBN-13: 978-1-58571-278-6
ISBN-10: 1-58571-278-7
$6.99

November

Yesterday Is Gone
Beverly Clark
ISBN-13: 978-1-58571-279-3
ISBN-10: 1-58571-279-5
$6.99

Again My Love
Kayla Perrin
ISBN-13: 978-1-58571-280-9
ISBN-10: 1-58571-280-9
$6.99

December

Office Policy
A.C. Arthur
ISBN-13: 978-1-58571-281-6
ISBN-10: 1-58571-281-7
$6.99

Rendezvous With Fate
Jeanne Sumerix
ISBN-13: 978-1-58571-283-3
ISBN-10: 1-58571-283-3
$6.99

2008 New Mass Market Titles

January

Where I Want To Be
Maryam Diaab
ISBN-13: 978-1-58571-268-7
ISBN-10: 1-58571-268-X
$6.99

Never Say Never
Michele Cameron
ISBN-13: 978-1-58571-269-4
ISBN-10: 1-58571-269-8
$6.99

February

Stolen Memories
Michele Sudler
ISBN-13: 978-1-58571-270-0
ISBN-10: 1-58571-270-1
$6.99

Dawn's Harbor
Kymberly Hunt
ISBN-13: 978-1-58571-271-7
ISBN-10: 1-58571-271-X
$6.99

March

Undying Love
Renee Alexis
ISBN-13: 978-1-58571-272-4
ISBN-10: 1-58571-272-8
$6.99

Blame It On Paradise
Crystal Hubbard
ISBN-13: 978-1-58571-273-1
ISBN-10: 1-58571-273-6
$6.99

April

When A Man Loves A Woman
La Connie Taylor-Jones
ISBN-13: 978-1-58571-274-8
ISBN-10: 1-58571-274-4
$6.99

Choices
Tammy Williams
ISBN-13: 978-1-58571-300-4
ISBN-10: 1-58571-300-7
$6.99

May

Dream Runner
Gail McFarland
ISBN-13: 978-1-58571-317-2
ISBN-10: 1-58571-317-1
$6.99

Southern Fried Standards
S.R. Maddox
ISBN-13: 978-1-58571-318-9
ISBN-10: 1-58571-318-X
$6.99

June

Looking for Lily
Africa Fine
ISBN-13: 978-1-58571-319-6
ISBN-10: 1-58571-319-8
$6.99

Bliss, Inc.
Chamein Canton
ISBN-13: 978-1-58571-325-7
ISBN-10: 1-58571-325-2
$6.99

2008 New Mass Market Titles (continued)

<u>July</u>

Love's Secrets
Yolanda McVey
ISBN-13: 978-1-58571-321-9
ISBN-10: 1-58571-321-X
$6.99

Things Forbidden
Maryam Diaab
ISBN-13: 978-1-58571-327-1
ISBN-10: 1-58571-327-9
$6.99

<u>August</u>

Storm
Pamela Leigh Starr
ISBN-13: 978-1-58571-323-3
ISBN-10: 1-58571-323-6
$6.99

Passion's Furies
AlTonya Washington
ISBN-13: 978-1-58571-324-0
ISBN-10: 1-58571-324-4
$6.99

<u>September</u>

Three Doors Down
Michele Sudler
ISBN-13: 978-1-58571-332-5
ISBN-10: 1-58571-332-5
$6.99

Mr Fix-It
Crystal Hubbard
ISBN-13: 978-1-58571-326-4
ISBN-10: 1-58571-326-0
$6.99

<u>October</u>

Moments of Clarity
Michele Cameron
ISBN-13: 978-1-58571-330-1
ISBN-10: 1-58571-330-9
$6.99

Lady Preacher
K.T. Richey
ISBN-13: 978-1-58571-333-2
ISBN-10: 1-58571-333-3
$6.99

<u>November</u>

This Life Isn't Perfect Holla
Sandra Foy
ISBN: 978-1-58571-331-8
ISBN-10: 1-58571-331-7
$6.99

Promises Made
Bernice Layton
ISBN-13: 978-1-58571-334-9
ISBN-10: 1-58571-334-1
$6.99

<u>December</u>

A Voice Behind Thunder
Carrie Elizabeth Greene
ISBN-13: 978-1-58571-329-5
ISBN-10: 1-58571-329-5
$6.99

The More Things Change
Chamein Canton
ISBN-13: 978-1-58571-328-8
ISBN-10: 1-58571-328-7
$6.99

Other Genesis Press, Inc. Titles

Other Genesis Press, Inc. Titles (continued)

Bodyguard	Andrea Jackson	$9.95
Boss of Me	Diana Nyad	$8.95
Bound by Love	Beverly Clark	$8.95
Breeze	Robin Hampton Allen	$10.95
Broken	Dar Tomlinson	$24.95
By Design	Barbara Keaton	$8.95
Cajun Heat	Charlene Berry	$8.95
Careless Whispers	Rochelle Alers	$8.95
Cats & Other Tales	Marilyn Wagner	$8.95
Caught in a Trap	Andre Michelle	$8.95
Caught Up In the Rapture	Lisa G. Riley	$9.95
Cautious Heart	Cheris F Hodges	$8.95
Chances	Pamela Leigh Starr	$8.95
Cherish the Flame	Beverly Clark	$8.95
Class Reunion	Irma Jenkins/	
	John Brown	$12.95
Code Name: Diva	J.M. Jeffries	$9.95
Conquering Dr. Wexler's Heart	Kimberley White	$9.95
Corporate Seduction	A.C. Arthur	$9.95
Crossing Paths, Tempting Memories	Dorothy Elizabeth Love	$9.95
Crush	Crystal Hubbard	$9.95
Cypress Whisperings	Phyllis Hamilton	$8.95
Dark Embrace	Crystal Wilson Harris	$8.95
Dark Storm Rising	Chinelu Moore	$10.95
Daughter of the Wind	Joan Xian	$8.95
Deadly Sacrifice	Jack Kean	$22.95
Designer Passion	Dar Tomlinson	$8.95
	Diana Richeaux	
Do Over	Celya Bowers	$9.95
Dreamtective	Liz Swados	$5.95

Other Genesis Press, Inc. Titles (continued)

Ebony Angel	Deatri King-Bey	$9.95
Ebony Butterfly II	Delilah Dawson	$14.95
Echoes of Yesterday	Beverly Clark	$9.95
Eden's Garden	Elizabeth Rose	$8.95
Eve's Prescription	Edwina Martin Arnold	$8.95
Everlastin' Love	Gay G. Gunn	$8.95
Everlasting Moments	Dorothy Elizabeth Love	$8.95
Everything and More	Sinclair Lebeau	$8.95
Everything but Love	Natalie Dunbar	$8.95
Falling	Natalie Dunbar	$9.95
Fate	Pamela Leigh Starr	$8.95
Finding Isabella	A.J. Garrotto	$8.95
Forbidden Quest	Dar Tomlinson	$10.95
Forever Love	Wanda Y. Thomas	$8.95
From the Ashes	Kathleen Suzanne	$8.95
	Jeanne Sumerix	
Gentle Yearning	Rochelle Alers	$10.95
Glory of Love	Sinclair LeBeau	$10.95
Go Gentle into that Good Night	Malcom Boyd	$12.95
Goldengroove	Mary Beth Craft	$16.95
Groove, Bang, and Jive	Steve Cannon	$8.99
Hand in Glove	Andrea Jackson	$9.95
Hard to Love	Kimberley White	$9.95
Hart & Soul	Angie Daniels	$8.95
Heart of the Phoenix	A.C. Arthur	$9.95
Heartbeat	Stephanie Bedwell-Grime	$8.95
Hearts Remember	M. Loui Quezada	$8.95
Hidden Memories	Robin Allen	$10.95
Higher Ground	Leah Latimer	$19.95
Hitler, the War, and the Pope	Ronald Rychiak	$26.95
How to Write a Romance	Kathryn Falk	$18.95

Other Genesis Press, Inc. Titles (continued)

Other Genesis Press, Inc. Titles (continued)

Other Genesis Press, Inc. Titles (continued)

Path of Fire	T.T. Henderson	$8.95
Path of Thorns	Annetta P. Lee	$9.95
Peace Be Still	Colette Haywood	$12.95
Picture Perfect	Reon Carter	$8.95
Playing for Keeps	Stephanie Salinas	$8.95
Pride & Joi	Gay G. Gunn	$8.95
Promises to Keep	Alicia Wiggins	$8.95
Quiet Storm	Donna Hill	$10.95
Reckless Surrender	Rochelle Alers	$6.95
Red Polka Dot in a World of Plaid	Varian Johnson	$12.95
Reluctant Captive	Joyce Jackson	$8.95
Rendezvous with Fate	Jeanne Sumerix	$8.95
Revelations	Cheris F. Hodges	$8.95
Rivers of the Soul	Leslie Esdaile	$8.95
Rocky Mountain Romance	Kathleen Suzanne	$8.95
Rooms of the Heart	Donna Hill	$8.95
Rough on Rats and Tough on Cats	Chris Parker	$12.95
Secret Library Vol. 1	Nina Sheridan	$18.95
Secret Library Vol. 2	Cassandra Colt	$8.95
Secret Thunder	Annetta P. Lee	$9.95
Shades of Brown	Denise Becker	$8.95
Shades of Desire	Monica White	$8.95
Shadows in the Moonlight	Jeanne Sumerix	$8.95
Sin	Crystal Rhodes	$8.95
Small Whispers	Annetta P. Lee	$6.99
So Amazing	Sinclair LeBeau	$8.95
Somebody's Someone	Sinclair LeBeau	$8.95
Someone to Love	Alicia Wiggins	$8.95
Song in the Park	Martin Brant	$15.95
Soul Eyes	Wayne L. Wilson	$12.95

Other Genesis Press, Inc. Titles (continued)

Other Genesis Press, Inc. Titles (continued)

Order Form

Mail to: Genesis Press, Inc.
P.O. Box 101
Columbus, MS 39703

Name _____
Address _____
City/State _____ Zip _____
Telephone _____

Ship to (if different from above)
Name _____
Address _____
City/State _____ Zip _____
Telephone _____

Credit Card Information
Credit Card # _____ ☐ Visa   ☐ Mastercard
Expiration Date (mm/yy) _____ ☐ AmEx   ☐ Discover

Qty.	Author	Title	Price	Total

Use this order

form, or call

1-888-INDIGO-1

Total for books _____
Shipping and handling:
 $5 first two books,
 $1 each additional book _____
Total S & H _____
Total amount enclosed _____
Mississippi residents add 7% sales tax